"A fine instructor she must be, not teaching her young ladies about the danger of rakes."

"School taught me everything I need to know, thank you."

"Everything, mon ange?" With that Corey drew her forward and brushed his other hand across her cheek and behind her head. He lowered his mouth to hers and kissed her, tenderly enough for his bruised lips, thoroughly enough to leave Melody dazed.

"Angel, Angel, you mustn't look at me all dewy and awestruck or I'll forget I am a gentleman altogether. It was only a simple kiss."

Her first rake. Her first kiss. The first time a second became eternity. And to him it was just a simple kiss? Melody sighed. "I suppose I have a lot to learn after all. . . ."

MINOR INDISCRETIONS

Barbara Metzger

FAWCETT CREST • NEW YORK

A Fawcett Crest Book
Published by Ballantine Books
Copyright © 1991 by Barbara Metzger

Library of Congress Catalog Card Number: 91-91818

ISBN 0-449-21872-4

Manufactured in the United States of America

First Edition: May 1991

This one is for Dottie,
Diane, Donna, and Eileen
with love

Chapter One

The bags were packed; the hired chaise waited
outside. It remained only to sit through the headmistress's parting speech, and Miss Melody Morley
Ashton would be free. After ten years of enforced
education, Melody had learned patience along with
grammar and globes, dance steps and deportment.
She sat in perfect dignity and composure, her back
straight, her fine green eyes lowered in respect,
prepared to swallow Miss Meadow's own blend of
tea (far superior to that served the students) along
with the old windbag's own brand of niggling nas-
tiness. Miss Meadow was small in stature, smaller
in mind, and smallest of all in human kindness,
according to the students at the Select Academy for
Young Ladies, located outside of Bath, which Melody would soon be leaving, praise be!

"All young things must eventually leave the
nest," the dumpy little matron recited, waving her
pudgy hands around. "They must try their wings,
take to the air."

The young woman on the other side of the desk

1

still wore a demure smile, wondering if Old Meadowlark was going to have her digging for her own worms before she was at last excused.

"Of course you are a trifle underage. We do prefer our young ladies to attend classes until they are eighteen. Those final courses in decorum are so crucial, don't you know."

Miss Ashton knew it nearly broke Miss Meadow's nipfarthing heart to return the unused tuition. As for the roll of guineas now wrapped in a handkerchief secured in Melody's reticule, tears had almost come to Miss Meadow's beady little eyes at having to hand over the money set aside for a student's incidental expenses.

"And yet, I do not feel I need worry about you casting shadows on the school's fine reputation. As I wrote to your dear mama, you have been one of our least troublesome, ah, best students. True, your musical abilities will never grace a drawing room, but that cannot be held against the school, now can it?" She tittered.

Melody tilted her head, her thick chestnut curls braided neatly into a coil at the back of her proudly held neck. She remembered agonizing, humiliating hours of practice, and folded her hands in her lap.

"No, as I told your mother, now that you have matured past a tendency to show inordinate temper, you are not one of the flighty girls with all their fits and starts who are no more suited to make an early debut in the ton than the cook's pot girl. I would be embarrassed to have some of them pitchforked into the haute monde. Poor reflection on the academy, don't you know." Miss Meadow plopped another almond tart into her pouched cheeks. "When your mother wrote that she wanted to introduce you at some small local gatherings and a house party or two before the Season officially started, I was not terribly concerned. After all, you will not be alone and untutored if you find yourself

2

at a loss in the wider range of polite society. Your mother will be there to guide you, and you must consider yourself fortunate indeed. Your mama turned out to be a fine lady. After a regrettable beginning, of course."

Ah, so there was to be a final examination after all. Miss Ashton bit down on her pride and temper, while Miss Meadow bit down on a macaroon. Melody nodded, her outward composure not touched by the gratuitous innuendo. Not after ten years.

She returned Miss Meadow's squinty black stare with a cool green gaze. "As you say, only the most narrow-minded of gossips would reflect on an age-old scandal. And Mother has certainly proven her gentility a hundredfold, not merely by being a cherished member of society, but with her truly noble charitable acts: running an entire orphanage by herself since Aunt Judith passed on, to say nothing of making a life for herself and her daughter with the passing of my father, and staying loyal to his memory. . . . I shall try very hard to live up to her good name."

Yes, Miss Ashton was mature beyond her seventeen years. If she could not be rattled by mention of the family's dirty linen, she would have no problems with those haughty Almack's patronesses and those other high-in-the-instep keepers of the ton whose approval was so necessary for a girl's success on the Marriage Mart. "Your own loyalty does you proud, my dear. Just maintain your values and the lessons we have drummed—ah, imparted to you, and do not let yourself be infected with all those romantic notions harum-scarum young girls are so prone to. Novels—" she shuddered at the word "—put more foolish ideas in more empty heads than a hundred teachers can displace in a lifetime. I am sure you will not succumb to such dire temptations."

Miss Ashton crossed her fingers and assured the

3

old besom that she wouldn't think of such a thing, aside from the four purple-bound volumes smuggled into her luggage by her classmates.

To guarantee that a promising young mind was not corrupted, at least until in her parent's care, Miss Meadow then handed a small book to Melody as a parting gift. No larger than her hand, it was a hefty little tome, with pearl-inlaid wooden covers, embossed gold corners, and sticky fingerprints.

"I am sure you will find it comforting and informative on your journey home. Please accept it with our very best wishes for your success."

Miss Ashton stood, her medium height at least six stately inches above the dumpy headmistress, and gave her best curtsy. Then she stuffed Mingleforth's *Rules of Polite Decorum* into her reticule, although the weight made the strings dig into her arm, and left before she was betrayed by a very girlish giggle indeed.

The bags were loaded; the hired chaise was off. Miss Melody Ashton tossed back the hood of her new velvet cape, green to match her eyes, and shook her head, loosening tiny reddish-brown curls to frame her cheeks.

"And good riddance," she shouted joyfully at her last glimpse of the ugly brick building. Then she quickly reached over to clasp her companion's hand. "I'm so sorry, Miss Chase. That was thoughtless of me, for you are not free of the place as I am."

Her fellow traveler, one of the younger instructors at the academy, begged her to pay no mind. "I cannot blame you for high spirits, my dear. I am only pleased I was selected to accompany you to your home. Even three days ..." She bit her lip, having said too much.

Melody squeezed the limp hand she held before sitting back on her own side of the carriage. "I know, I shall ask Mama if you cannot accompany

4

us when we go up to London. She won't want to visit the Tower or Westminster or all the lending libraries I am anxious to see, and I cannot go by myself, of course. It will be perfect."

"Yes, dear," Miss Chase answered without conviction, five years at Miss Meadow's having left her with little hope and fewer dreams. The expectation of days in a jouncing carriage, indifferent food, and unaired sheets at various inns, and then a return journey alone on the mail coach, was a positive treat compared to a junior mistress's life at the school. She was happy enough to sink into an exhausted slumber.

Left to her own devices, Melody untied her reticule's strings and, with a smile that showed one quicksilver dimple, drew forth Miss Meadow's gift and read the inscription inside the front cover: *The child who is shown the path, and knows the path, will follow the path.* She chuckled softly, thinking of primrose paths and paths to hell. Trust Miss Meadow to adopt addlepated profundity when *With our best wishes* would have done. Melody closed the book and fumbled with the window latch.

"Oh no, my dear, you mustn't," Miss Chase murmured.

"But I was just going to—"

"The dust from the road and the cold, you know." Miss Chase shivered in her threadbare pelisse.

Melody hurriedly fastened the window and tucked the lap robe around her companion, who promptly closed her eyes again. Melody ruefully stuffed Mingleforth's *Rules of Polite Decorum* back into her overloaded purse. Perhaps it would come in handy someday for propping up a chair leg, or providing kindling, or lining a canary's cage. Not that Miss Ashton owned a canary, but she had always hoped to. She had always hoped for pretty gowns, balls, and jewels, putting her hair up, sipping champagne, and meeting the Prince. She pulled her cape closer around her and settled into her own comfortable corner, her green eyes drifting shut, a smile on her pretty face.

For Melody Morley Ashton, levelheaded, dignified, and mature, had more than a few romantic notions. A love match, that's where her dreams always led. She knew she was supposed to marry well; what girl at Miss Meadow's didn't know the point of her existence? Each proper female's mission was to add consequence to her family, to join her name to someone with a higher title or deeper pockets, preferably both. That fact of life was taught to even the youngest pupil, along with drawing room accomplishments, and everything and anything to attract this most eligible of *partis*.

Let him be wealthy and well connected, Melody prayed, but mostly let me love him. Let me know a grand passion, like Mama.

Of course, Melody did not wish to marry a ne'erdo-well, sporting-mad gambler as her mother had. She barely remembered her handsome father, dead on a muddy field due to too high a fence and too deep a bottle, leaving her and her mother impoverished. But at least her mother had had her grand passion, a runaway match, a love that survived parental disapproval and society's strictures, if not an unbroken gelding. Lord Ashton's untimely death—and unpaid bills—had left his wife and young child homeless and hopeless.

Please, let him not be a second son, Melody's prayers continued.

Lady Jessamyn Ashton's only course was to throw herself and Melody on the untender mercies of her much older sister, Judith Morley, a moralistic, man-hating spinster who had inherited the Oaks, the Morley ancestral home at Copley-Whitmore. Aunt Judith devoted her life to good deeds and her ward Felice, the daughter of Sir Bostwick Bartleby, the nabob. Felice devoted her

6

life to making Melody miserable. Felice was two years older, china doll pretty, and graceful. Melody was sallow faced then, scrawny, and awkward. She was a brown study, quiet child. Blond-haired Felice was not.

"Your papa gambled all his money away; *my* papa is in India, adding to his fortune. You'll have no dowry; I'll have diamonds and rubies and pearls. You'll marry a farmer; I'll marry a maharajah, if I choose."

Somehow Lady Ashton found enough money to send Melody to school, and somehow she found the means to reenter society, floating from country house party to Irish hunt meeting, from seashore excursion to London Season, during Melody's vacations at the Oaks or not. Even after Aunt Judith's death, Lady Jessamyn continued her social rounds and yet maintained Judith's good works. Melody dreamed of making her mother proud, this mother she hardly knew, who was everything a lady should be.

Now was Melody's chance to have it all, the Season, her mama's company, true love. Unfortunately, Felice was waiting with Mama at the Oaks.

So let him not prefer blondes.

Chapter Two

$\mathcal{D}$aydreams are peculiar, taking on lives of their own. Think of the inveterate gambler who is positive his horse will win the next time. He'll lay all his blunt on the nag, even borrow on his optimism. He'll decide to pay off his bills, treat himself to a fine dinner on the winnings, even hand his wife a few of the flimsies, maybe. The money is all spent before the horses leave the starting line. Just so, by the next morning Miss Ashton was the Season's Incomparable, the belle of every ball, in her mind's eye. London beaux were at her feet writing sonnets to her eyebrows, while one gentleman in particular . . .

As for Miss Chase, the downtrodden, colorless schoolteacher, she was delighted with an ample, hot meal at last night's inn, and the fact that there were no creatures sharing her bed.

So the next morning, who was most devastated by the change in plans? On being informed that she was to return to Bath with the hired chaise, Miss Chase was only mildly affected. She would miss another day or two of freedom, but she was richer by a good night's rest, a full breakfast, and two of Miss Ashton's precious guineas. Perhaps she was correct: hope for little, and you won't be disappointed.

For there, at the first change, along with Mama's note that Melody should proceed in the family carriage, was the death of all her fantasies. This killer of dreams, slayer of wishes, sat like a dark specter in the inn's parlor: Nanny. Melody's nanny, her mother's nanny, perhaps Queen Guinevere's nanny, she'd been at it so long. Nanny in her starched black gown, black bonnet, black mustache, with her ubiquitous knitting, was truly the hangman of hope.

"Cow's dry. Well's dry. You be wanted to home."

Doom.

The bags were unloaded; the hired chaise pulled away.

"Nanny?"

"Money's gone. Can't get blood from a turnip, I says."

"From a stone, Nanny. You cannot get blood from a stone. But what—"

Nanny shook her head and kept on knitting. "All that learning. A body can't eat stones, missy. Nor books nor fine ideas. Head as hard as rocks. Hard times."

"Do you mean we're . . . poor?"

"We were always poor. What's worse than poor?"

"But, but Mama and the orphans and—"

"Your mama's in a decline, children running wild. Servants gone. Constable's nosing round. We'll be digging acorns next, I told her. Tried eating toads, missy?" At Melody's gasp she guessed not. "Bein't all bad, howsomever. Some of us got our health. Not Ducky nor little Meggie, a course, who's never been a strong 'un, and some of the boys is sniffling. Your ma hardly gets out of bed these days. Then there's my rheumatics and—"

9

"But what happened? What about all the plans for house parties and a London Season?" Melody plucked at the folds of her new, expensive cape. "My new clothes?"

Nanny turned her nose up at the green velvet. "Here, you'll need this."

This was a wool scarf she uncoiled like a rope from her workbasket and wrapped around Melody's throat. It was that same scratchy, undyed wool Nanny always used, with the smell of sheep still in it. Melody could feel rashes on her chin already. "But—"

"Air dreams, your mama always had her head filled with air dreams. She'll tell you. You're needed to home, is all I'm supposed to say." And Nanny pursed her lips, gathered up her knitting, and stomped out the door.

Heaven help us, the bags were being loaded. The rickety, ramshackle, crumbly old family carriage stood waiting. In Melody's memory only chickens had used it, for roosting. The neighborhood of Copley-Whitmore was small enough to get everywhere on foot, and Aunt Judith had been a firm believer in healthful exercise—rain, sleet, or snow. An ancient driver was at the reins, muffled to the eyes in another undyed wool scarf.

"Isn't that old Toby from Tucker's farm? Why, he's more used to driving—" Yes, now that she looked closer, those were indeed plow horses between the traces, huge, placid beasts that had one gait, a ponderous, plodding walk. "Why, it will take forever to get home behind those animals."

The old man cackled. "Aye, but they'll go in the prettiest, straightest line you ever seen." Then he scratched his chin.

At least she was not going to hell in a handcart, Melody decided, wrinkling her nose. She was getting there slower, in a henhouse on wheels.

10

The horses plowed on. Urging Toby to greater speed was fruitless, for the old man was quite deaf when it suited him. Nanny knitted, like the Fates weaving Melody's future in itchy skeins. There was no budging Nanny from her decision to stay mumchance on everything Melody wanted to know either. Conjecture was pointless, so Melody tried to settle back on the odoriferous squabs, but loose horsehair stuffing kept pricking into her back, and the badly sprung carriage kept rocking her head and shoulder into the unpadded door. Life at Miss Meadow's was taking on a rosier cast.

At least they would not starve. Nanny had brought a huge hamper of food along, filled with fresh bread, cold chicken, thick chunks of cheese, apples, a jug of cider, and even Melody's favorite gingerbread.

"There's so much here, Nanny; surely your tales of woe must be exaggerated," Melody noted hopefully.

"Out of the mouths of babes . . ."

Melody stopped chewing. "You cannot mean the children are going hungry? I couldn't eat another morsel if I thought so."

Her chick withering away without proper nourishment? Nanny relented. "Nay, we brought our own rather than pay ransom prices for a bit of victuals from those highway robbers pretending to be honest innkeeps. Dirty hands they have, too; you never know if they be mucking stables or serving dinner." Nanny bit into an apple. "At least I know whose orchard these were stole from."

Melody choked.

Needless to say, the travelers were treated less than royally at the inn where they spent the night. The women would not order dinner, and the horses did not require changing or a postboy's attentions, just feed and a rest. And not only did Nanny haggle with the owner over the price of a room, but she

11

accused the poor man of watering the wine, brewing the tea leaves thrice over, making improper advances to his serving girls, and burying the bones of unwary wayfarers out back. And she did all this, standing as rigid as a masthead on a man-of-war, in the only public room the inn offered, in full view and hearing of two local dairymen, a merchant of some sort in a checkered waistcoat, and a party of four rowdy young bucks on their way to a mill.

Melody pulled her cape's hood down over her eyes and prayed for a bolt of lightning. Instead she got snickers and guffaws and the tiniest of attic rooms with the narrowest of thin mattresses, which she was to share with Nanny. There was not even a chair, nor room to sleep on the floor. There was no hot water to wash in, which really was all of a piece, for Nanny would not let her change into her nightclothes, or sleep beneath the covers. Who knew what pox-ridden fiend slept there last?

Not Miss Ashton, that was for sure, cold and crammed between Nanny's angular bulk and the even more rigid wall, listening to the raucous young men in the taproom and Nanny's snores.

The following day dawned cold, cloudy, and very, very early. Workhorses rise with the sun. So, it seems, do disgruntled innkeepers who see no reason to cater to jug-bitten nobs who take to smashing chairs, toplofty old harridans with tongues like vipers, or schoolgirls who really should have had more beauty sleep.

Miss Ashton needed a hot bath, her morning chocolate, and someone to help braid her thick hair. What she got was advice: "Don't you go putting on airs like some I could mention."

So cold wash water it was. Then Nanny took the brush and scraped it through Melody's hair like a garden hoe through creepers. Melody hurriedly tied her hair back in a ribbon while she still had any,

12

and straightened her dress as much as possible. Nanny retied her muffler, despite Melody's protests, saying, "Fresh air is what you need to get rid of that peaked look."

"Nanny, I'm a grown woman now. You can't keep treating me like an unruly child!"

"Humph. Birds don't fall far from the tree."

"That's apples, Nanny."

"If you want apples to break your fast, that's fine with me, Miss Book-Learning. I'd just as soon not give that thief another groat for lumpy porridge."

Old Bess and Thimble were right fresh, Toby informed them. "They'll be setting a lively pace this morning, see if they don't."

"Maybe they could be encouraged into a trot now and then, do you think? Nothing that might tire them out, of course."

Toby cupped his hand to his ear. "What's that, miss?"

Melody gave up and took a deep breath of the last unfouled air she would get for a while. She smiled that it should be *unfowled*, and climbed into her seat across from Nanny. The bread was not quite as fresh this morning, and the cider was a touch vinegary, but at least her hunger was satisfied. Melody's need for sleep came next. She made herself as comfortable as possible, using her hood as a pillow, and drowsed off to the steady clops of the horses, the sway of the carriage, and the click of Nanny's needles.

She awoke to angry shouts and curses, and Nanny's hands clapped painfully over her ears.

The horses were keeping their steady pace, it seemed, straight and true down the center of the road, to the disgust of other travelers.

"Halloo, the carriage! Move off to the side, blast you, and let someone pass. By all that's holy, you don't own the whole bloody highway!"

Toby was still deaf this morning. Nanny put her

13

head out of the window and shouted back, "You ought to have your mouth washed out with soap, young jackanapes. This is the King's highway, and there be ladies present."

That carriage passed them, two of its wheels dangerously close to the ditch, and then a few others went by, sporting vehicles with raffish young gentlemen at the ribbons, from what Melody could see from her position, scrunched down in her seat as small as possible. It wouldn't matter if there was no money for a London Season; her chances there would be immediately ruined if any of these town-bronzed gentlemen recognized her.

The next voices on the road behind were familiar. The four revelers from last night's inn were on the road earlier than usual, before they'd had a chance to sleep off the evening's effects. They had just completed their private wagers on the coming mill, so quite naturally, by these bloods' standards, the only thing left to enliven the drive to West Fenton was a contest between their two racing curricles. It made no matter that the roadway was becoming crowded with other vehicles headed for the same destination, or oncoming traffic, or farmers herding sheep by the verge, or the great lumbering relic of a coach. It certainly never occurred to any of the young gents that their judgment might be the slightest diminished.

"It's the old hag from the inn," called out the driver of the leading carriage to his passenger's, "Tallyho!" The other curricle drew neck and neck, and Miss Ashton could hear bets being laid, wild sums being wagered on which vehicle could pass the old coach first. They both pulled wide, to either side of Melody's carriage.

Melody tried to shout to Toby to pull over, but Nanny was waving her knitting out the window and ranting about how someone should take sticks to such care-for-naughts.

14

"Catch the prize!" one driver roared, while his whooping passenger leaned dizzyingly off the edge of his seat.

"Twenty guineas more if you can snabble it!" came from the other side.

Melody shut her eyes. Nanny squawked. There was an ominous crunch as one of the curricle's wheels scraped by, and then the old coach came to such a quick halt that Melody was thrown forward right off her seat, onto the floor that was still littered with chicken droppings.

Now Old Bess and Thimble knew their job. If there was a rabbit in the field, it was the rabbit's job to scamper off. If the plow was stuck on a rock, it was Toby's job to free it. They weren't bothered by silly fools darting by, or loud laughter, or even Nanny's squalls of divine retribution. But snakes, long, flappy white snakes trailing across their backs—that was not their job. They whoaed all right, with another crunch of the wooden axle.

Nanny stood clutching her empty workbag, shaking her head in disbelief, while Toby and Melody walked around the carriage.

"Wheel's took a whack, I swear, no telling if it'll last. Axle's got a crack, prob'ly. Worse, horses is spooked. These two ain't going to budge right aways. I know them. After a bit, maybe we could go real slow, see if she holds."

Slower than they'd been going? "Perhaps you should walk ahead and send a blacksmith back," Melody suggested.

"What's that, miss? You and Nanny want to step along to the village coming up? That's a fine idea, ma'am. Could be hours else, and you'd likely have to walk it anyway, if t'wheel comes off. There's a posting house on the square, so there's bound to be a smith. I'll just give Old Bess and Thimble here a chance at some of that new spring grass, then be along after you."

15

In little under an hour, Toby caught up, leading the pair, the coach creaking behind. Just when the road was really congested with all manner of sporting gentlemen heading for West Fenton and the mill, Melody's little procession wended its slow way onward, following the path of—and meticulously rewinding—a thread of hoof-marked, mud-caked, crinkled wool.

Chapter Three

$\mathcal{T}$his time Melody was determined to get to the innkeeper first. It was the innkeeper's wife, though, who spied the bedraggled group entering her establishment and sent her husband away to tend to the crowded taproom. In Mamie Barstow's experience, sporting nobs always attracted a certain type of women, and she wasn't having any of it, not at her inn. She stood guarding the front door, arms folded across her chest.

"Good day, ma'am," Melody began. "Your inn looks to be a pleasant place, and my companion and I are sorely in need of rest and refreshment. I hope that you can accommodate us."

On closer examination, Mrs. Barstow recognized quality. The young woman with such cultured accents was standing proud as a queen, just as if she didn't look like she'd been dragged through a hedge backward, and the companion was brandishing a knitting needle aloft like a saber charge. The old wreck of a carriage would have been in fashion thirty years ago, but the driver would have been old even then. Whatever this odd lot was, they weren't loose women; light-skirts fared better. Still, they did not belong at her inn, not today.

"I'm sorry, miss, but you can see there's a big to-do this afternoon. The place is overbooked as it is, and some of the gentlemen are like to get above themselves, if you know what I mean."

Nanny snorted. "Hanging's too good for the likes of them. Attacking honest women in broad daylight. Ravaging the countryside. Spare the rod, and use a butcher's knife, I say."

Mrs. Barstow's mouth hung open, and the door was about to shut. Melody quickly withdrew the roll of coins from her reticule. As she unwrapped her bona fides she raised her chin. "I believe some of your guests are already castaway, but we have no choice. There has been a mishap with the carriage, and we are left here until it can be repaired."

"Oh dear, and no work likely to get done soon, with every man jack in the town out to watch the fight. Still, every bed is spoken for, and some doubled as it is."

"Heathens," Nanny muttered.

"Please, ma'am, we just require a quiet place away from the public view." Melody jingled a few coins together.

"I suppose I could let you have our own rooms for a bit. Mr. Barstow can bunk with the stable lads, and I'll share with the maids, for all the sleep we'll be getting this night. It won't be what you're used to, I swear, but you'll be safer here than out on the road."

Melody was used to sharing a room with four other girls; last night she'd shared a bed with Nanny. "I'm sure that will be fine."

"And mind, I haven't got a spare girl to be fetching and carrying for you, and I'll be too busy cooking and serving, what with all these gentlemen to feed."

18

Nanny puckered up her mouth as if she had swallowed a lemon. "No way I'd let some tavern wench take care of my chick." Melody quickly added another coin to the handful she rattled.

"There's some pigeon pie left from luncheon, nothing fancy. And there's always stew and a kettle on for tea. I suppose it will do, if you just stay out of the public rooms."

Nanny swore to lock the windows, put chairs across the doors, lay her body across the sill if need be, to keep her lady in and all the depraved sons of Satan out. Shaking her head, Mrs. Barstow led them down the hall past the taproom. Nanny pulled Melody's hood so far down over her eyes she couldn't see, and so as a result nearly stumbled right into a broad gentleman in a spotted Belcher tie. He put up a quizzing glass and asked, "What have we here?" He got an enlarged eyeful of Nanny's Gorgon glare and a sharp knitting needle in his breadbasket.

Mrs. Barstow hustled them through the dining room, thankfully empty now, and beyond into the kitchen where two young girls in neat aprons were peeling vegetables. Past the pantry was a half landing and there, to everyone's relief, was the door leading to a tiny sitting room with a sofa and chair, and an even smaller bedroom. Mrs. Barstow twitched a faded quilt into place on the bed, and Nanny pulled all the curtains closed. Soon there was food and blessedly hot water and Nanny's snores almost drowning out the commotion in the taproom and the rattle of pots and pans in the kitchen.

Melody spent some time trying to sponge off her cape and unsnarl her hair before lying down to nap. Her mind was too unsettled, though, and the noises were getting louder and more distracting. She wished she had her luggage from the carriage so she could change her gown, or at least retrieve one of those Minerva Press novels from her trunk. Perhaps if she could just locate Toby in the yard, she could find out how long repairs would take or if he could fetch in the bags. Mrs. Barstow was still in the kitchen, however, up to her arms in pastry dough. She waved the rolling pin in the air and gave Melody such a scowl that the younger woman scurried back to her rooms. Maybe she could spot Toby from the window and get his attention.

When she opened the curtains in the sitting room, Melody had to take her shoes off and stand on the sofa to see out, the window being so high. Because the little apartment was up a landing, she found herself looking down on the inn's rear courtyard, with stable blocks forming the other three sides to the square, and, good grief, the entire clearing was filled with shouting, shoving men! She leaped off the sofa. What if anyone looked up and saw her?

Don't be a goose, she told herself, they are all more interested in what's going on than in looking around at the scenery. Furthermore, enough of them must have seen her walking at the head of her little caravan en route to the inn for her to be a laughingstock as it was. So just what *was* going on? She hopped back up.

One man was standing in an open area at the center of the courtyard, ringed by rough wooden benches all filled with workingmen in coarse smocks sitting next to gentlemen in lace-edged linens. Behind them stood more so-called sportsmen, and in the last rows the carriages were arranged, with the Corinthians in their top hats and many-caped driving coats looking down on the proceedings from their lofty perches. Melody could not pinpoint the two racing curricles from the morning anywhere; perhaps they had landed in a ditch. She did see serving girls carrying trays of mugs, and men collecting sheaves of paper, and one person in a frieze coat making marks on a big board.

And still the man in the clearing stood curiously alone.

He was an enormous man, she could see even from this distance, with a red face and black mustachio. The crowd roared when he took off his leather jerkin and shook one huge fist at them. The muscles in his arms and chest poured over each other in layers, dark, hairy, sweat-dampened layers. What an education Miss Melody was getting!

"Al-bert," the crowd chanted, "Al-bert." Albert, obviously the local favorite, circled his little clearing, waving. Then he stood, his hands on his wide hips, waiting. And waiting some more. The noises from the benches grew louder, with whistles and foot-stampings joining the shouts. Some of the men started tossing their mugs at one another. Scuffles broke out, and the serving girls ran back toward the kitchen, screeching. The man Melody identified as the innkeeper, the one wearing an apron and tearing his hair out, tried to separate the brawlers and get others back in their seats.

Then, when it looked like the inn yard would turn into a free-for-all, a stern voice that was obviously used to command called "Halt!" There was a moment of silence, and Melody could see a high-crowned beaver hat come gliding into the clearing next to Albert. It was easy to tell where the hat had come from: all heads were turned toward the back where a gentleman was standing in an elegant high-perch phaeton. He was handing his coat to his companion, untying his neckcloth as he stepped down from the carriage as casually as if he were going for a stroll in the park. He was fair-haired and tanned and, although the distance was too great, Melody just knew he was bound to be handsome, with such assurance.

The crowd took up a new chant now: "Cor-ey, Cor-ey, Cor-ey," and she lost sight of him in the mobs. When he reappeared, he was stripped to his boots and buckskins, and Melody was right. He was beautiful. Where Albert was all hulking thew and flab, Corey was like a Greek god in a garden, rock hard, sculpted, sun kissed.

He was also inches shorter than Albert and half his girth. He was going to get killed.

As the two men squared off with their fists raised, and the chanting turned to a thunderous uproar, Melody scrambled down from her perch. She went into the bedroom where Nanny still slept, shut the door, got into bed, and pulled the quilt over her head.

Chapter Four

"*H*ere you go, my lord, nice and easy now. You can rest here, private like."

"Mmunh . . . wife . . ."

"Never you mind the missus. She's just in a pother, what with all the argle-bargle. Feared for her rug, likely, is why she kicked up a dust about me bringin' you in here. You, uh, ain't about to cast up accounts, are you?"

"Hunh . . ."

"Good, good. Don't worry over my Mamie. Nothin's too good for you, and I'll tell her so. Saved my bacon, you did, my lord. They would have torn the place to splinters when the Irishman didn't show. You just lie back now whilst I go send a boy off for the doctor. Be here before the cat can lick its ear. I'll fetch some towels and hot water, meanwhile. We'll have you right as a trivet, my lord, don't you fret."

"Mumunh?"

"Brandy? Of course, my lord. Nothing but the best for you."

Mr. Barstow left, and Melody checked to make

23

sure Nanny was still sleeping. Then she tiptoed to the bedroom door and ever so quietly opened it a crack to peep out. Mr. Corey—Lord Corey, it seemed, which she should have guessed—was sprawled out on the sofa, what was left of him anyway. He had survived, but barely, from the looks of it. His blond hair was plastered to his forehead in damp curls, blood was dribbling down one brow into an eye already swelling shut, and he held a length of cloth, likely his neckpiece, over his nose. That was why she could not hear his words to the innkeeper, Melody realized, her eyes traveling lower. Lord Corey's shirt was draped over his broad shoulders, trailing in streams of blood, some dried, some not, which ran between huge red welts on his chest and down his sides. His buckskin breeches were blood spattered and torn, one knee shredded.

Melody shuddered and closed the door. Then he moaned, and she peeked out again.

Lord Corey took the cloth away from his nose—it was soaked through anyway—and muttered. "Hell and damnation," Melody could hear quite distinctly. "No reason to get blood all over the woman's couch." He levered himself up and took one cautious step toward the wooden chair before his foot skidded on something. Lord Corey fell, hitting his head soundly on the pine end table.

"Blast!" he swore, rubbing the back of his head and then grabbing for the sodden linen when his nose started gushing again. Still on the floor, Corey reached behind him for what had tripped him: Melody's slipper. "What the bloody hell—"

Melody just had to go to him. He obviously needed help, but not as much as he would need if Nanny woke up and found a half-naked man spouting blasphemy in the sitting room. Another round with Albert would be a waltz by comparison.

She only stopped to snatch up her reticule with the extra handkerchiefs and the vinaigrette Miss

24

Meadow insisted the girls carry, before softly pulling the door shut behind her. "Ssh," Melody whispered.

"Who the—?" Only one blue eye opened, but what a sight it beheld! Lord Corey, better known as Lord Cordell Inscoe, Viscount Coe, looked up to see a shapely young woman in a high-waisted sprigged muslin gown, with dark hair that curled in red and gold flickers around soft, peach-tinged cheeks, and eyes so green they should belong to a mermaid or a forest dryad or . . . He held up the slipper in his hand and noted her stockinged feet. "Cinderella. Ah, and I am not dressed for the ball." To use boxing cant, Lord Coe had been tipped another settler.

He tried to rise, to gather his shirt closed, to dab at the warm blood on his upper lip. With Melody's help, he made it to the chair, but he had to sit still a moment, gasping and clutching his ribs, and her hand. Melody stared around desperately. She couldn't just leave an injured man, could she? Even Nanny must see that.

Mr. Barstow saw it when he brought a loaded tray into the room. "Lawkes, where'd she come from?"

"Heaven, my good man, heaven. Where else would an angel come from?"

"Well, there'll be hell to pay, an' my wife catches you at it."

Melody resented that. "I'll have you know, sir, that Mrs. Barstow herself was kind enough to permit me and my companion the use of these rooms." She nodded her head toward the adjoining room, as if another closed door would prove her respectability when a bare-chested man held her hand in his.

Barstow scratched his head. "I don't know. She said somethin', but with all the commotion in the kitchen . . ."

Corey took over. "Come now, man. I'm in no shape for anything your wife would disapprove. I

25

only ravish maidens on Fridays. Wednesdays are my days for being beaten to a pulp. And you can see that Miss—ah, the young lady is properly reared and properly chaperoned." He, too, nodded to the other door, having no idea whatsoever who or what was behind it. "So why don't you pour me a glass of that fine brandy I see there, and then go on back to tend to all of the pub business before your clientele decides to reenact that last round in your common room?"

"But you need doctorin'. Our local sawbones might take a while to get here, it seems. Martin Reilly's wife, you know. Jake the ostler's a dab hand with injuries, howsomever. He'll be glad to strap them ribs up for you."

Corey tossed back the glass and held it out for more. "Thank you, friend, but I'll wait for the doctor."

"I got some salve for them cuts, my lord. I'll just—"

"From Jake the stableman?"

Melody was already dipping one of the towels into the can of hot water and gingerly dabbing at his forehead. "My angel's ministrations will be a lot more tender than yours, Barstow. Go feed the masses, fill the coffers." Glass broke somewhere down the hall. "Save the good bottles."

Barstow backed out of the room quickly, and Melody continued with the towels and water and salve. "I am, you know," she said quietly, pushing his head back and laying a dampened cloth across the bridge of his nose, which was still bleeding slightly.

"You are what, *mon ange*?"

"Properly reared and properly chaperoned."

"I never doubted it for a moment. Of course, I have never known a chaperone to be so accommodatingly invisible, or a debutante to go barefoot at her come-out ball—Ouch!"

26

"I'm sorry, my lord. Did I hurt you? I think this should be stitched. Perhaps Jake . . . ?"

"You've made your point, Miss—Ah, our host seems to have failed to make the formal introduction. No, don't say anything; it's all to the good. You may find the need someday to deny the association. This way I can swear I never met any Miss So and So, only a kind-hearted seraph."

"Silly, I know you are Lord Corey."

Few people had ever called the viscount silly. Fewer had fussed over him with such sweet, selfless concern. "My friends call me Corey."

"You seemed to have a great many out there shouting for you."

"I just had better odds. The underdog, you know."

She was concentrating on getting a sticking plaster to his forehead, her tongue between her teeth. He never felt the pain. She did, and her eyes grew moist.

"What's this, Angel, tears? Don't worry, head wounds just bleed a lot."

"That's not it. All those people were *cheering* while you were getting hurt."

He touched her cheek with a bruised knuckle. "An angel, indeed."

"No, I'm not," she said angrily, trying to get the dried blood off his chin, which she could see was very strong and square. "It's just that you were so . . . so . . . handsome is not the right word. A lot of men are handsome. You were perfect, like some kind of hero. Now look at you!"

Melody felt herself blushing. However could she have said that to him, a total stranger?

Corey had forgotten such innocence still existed. His heart thumped—or was that just a twinge from a cracked rib? He smiled as best he could with a swollen lip. "Well, I'll admit I am not a pretty sight right now, sweetheart, but I doubt any of the mess is permanent. The ribs are the worst of it, and

27

they'll heal. I still have all my teeth, and if that doctor does a halfway decent job of stitching, there won't be much of a scar on my brow. It wouldn't be the first anyway, after the cavalry." He moved the cloth and carefully touched his nose. "Luckiest of all, my nose isn't even broken."

"As if that makes it right!"

His nose had finally stopped bleeding; his eye needed a slab of liver or something. Her inspection continued down—No, mopping at a man's chest was still beyond her daring. She'd never even seen one before today! For goodness' sake, she'd never been alone in a room with a man before today. Melody dragged her eyes back to Corey's, and caught an amused, knowing smile. She took his hand and poured brandy over the torn knuckles.

"The deuce!"

"Sorry, my lord, but spirits are the best thing to keep a wound from infection."

"And a waste of fine liquor. I can see by that martial look in your eye that you disagree and are about to do your worst to my other poor hand. Do you think I might have another glass while there is a drop left?"

Her hand shook slightly when she poured, he noticed, along with noticing the graceful tilt of her neck, the soft curve of her gown's bodice. His own hand shook slightly. "Perhaps you should have a sip also. This cannot be pleasant for you."

"Thank you, my lord, but I am not used to spirits."

"I'll warrant you aren't used to nursing fallen gladiators, either. You have my gratitude, of course, and also my respect. Every other young lady I know would have fainted long ago, and some gentlemen, too."

"Paltry fellows," she said, to cover her embarrassment at his praise. She certainly could not admit to the queasy feeling in her stomach. "And

28

Monday is my day to be a vaporish female, not Wednesday."

His hands were dried and loosely wrapped in torn strips of linen. That left his chest to be tended, his taut-skinned, well-muscled chest. Melody took a deep breath.

Corey chuckled. "Are you sure you wouldn't like a drink? Dutch courage, don't you know."

He was altogether too knowing.

"I'm, ah, afraid of hurting you further. Shouldn't you do this?"

He held up his bandaged hands and just smiled. The dratted man was enjoying her discomfort.

"Ow!"

"Sorry."

"Like hell you are."

Maybe if she distracted him, and herself, she could consider this just another job, like polishing silver or rinsing a fragile teapot. Of course no teapot of her experience had soft golden hairs or firm—

"Why did you do it? I mean the, ah, fight. It could not have been for the money, I know." At his raised eyebrow, the good one, she admitted to spying out the window and seeing his expensive equipage. Then there were his clothes, and the deference of Mr. Barstow.

"Have you never heard of punting on tick, little one? No, I can see from your face you haven't. No matter, I am well enough to pass that I need not hire myself out for a sparring partner. And no, I am not so noble a character to sacrifice myself to save Mr. Barstow's inn from an ugly melee. It was the challenge of the thing. The locals were boasting that Irish Red had gone fainthearted, and no one could best Albert. I took the dare."

"You did this for a *dare*?" She rubbed more vigorously; the viscount clenched his teeth. "Of all the irresponsible, reckless, cork-brained notions. Isn't that just like a man."

"How much could you know about men, from your great age? What are you anyway, eighteen, nineteen?"

Melody chose not to answer that. "I know that my father was just such a one, gambling on duck races, taking every madcap challenge, thinking no farther than the excitement of the moment! Why, you could have been killed!"

"So little faith, my angel. But I did weigh my chances, you know. After all, there is science involved. Albert is the product of barroom brawls, while I have studied with Gentleman Jackson. Albert had strength, I knew, but I had speed. He may have the brawn, but I have the brains."

"And the conceit! I should have thought the brains of a flea would tell you not to get in the ring with a man twice your size. Just look at you!"

"Ah, but you haven't seen Albert."

"You mean you won?"

Her look of incredulity struck a blow to his pride, possibly the only part of the viscount not yet injured. Then she smiled, with dimples and sparkling eyes, and it was almost worth it, even the aching ribs. Gads, what a little beauty! Young and unsophisticated, she was unaware of her effect on a man, if Corey knew women at all—and he knew women as well as he knew the art of boxing. She wasn't in his line, of course. Unless a man was on the Marriage Mart, schoolroom misses, debutantes, and such were like playing with fire. Corey much preferred to dally with women who already smoldered. But if, say, a man was thirty-five or so—the viscount was only twenty-eight—and he was looking to get legshackled, a fellow could do a lot worse.

As it was, sea-green eyes, adorable dimples, and petal-soft skin were exactly why chaperones were created. Which reminded him that his angel's was not doing a very good job of it. "I'll, ah, take over from here," he said, chivalrously relieving her of

30

the towel, and himself of dangerous thoughts as she wiped at the red streaks lower down his chest.

"I don't mean to sound ungrateful or anything, but isn't your companion being a trifle lax?"

"Nanny's nerves were overset so she took a sleeping draught, thank goodness. I mean, she needs her rest. There was a mishap with the carriage, and we had to walk a considerable distance this morning."

"Never tell me you are the Incognita in the ancient coach the fellows were snickering about before? They were calling you the Damsel, the Dragon, and Dobbin. That was you?" He laughed out loud, then clutched his side. "Dash it, I shouldn't have laughed."

Melody's chin was raised. Her tone was grim, "No, sir, you shouldn't have."

"Now you are angry. I'm truly sorry, Angel, really I am. Tell me what I can do to make things right."

How could she not forgive a silver-tongued devil with a ready smile and a black eye? She tugged his shirt around him better. "So you won't take a chill. And thank you, but unless you can play Cinderella's fairy godmother, wave your wand, and get my carriage fixed in a hurry, I don't think there is much you can do for me."

He laughed again, but much more cautiously. "I'm afraid I'll stay in your black books then, my dear, for your carriage won't be repaired anytime soon. Albert is the blacksmith!"

Chapter Five

*T*he doctor came. Melody vanished into the bedroom.

It was a good thing Nanny had a heavy hand with the laudanum. And a good thing the doctor had some experience with ex-soldiers and dockworkers, or other patients with colorful vocabularies. And it was an especially good thing that Melody, behind the bedroom door, did not understand half of what she heard. No maiden's education need be *that* complete.

The doctor left, and Barstow and one of his stable lads helped Lord Corey down the hall, out of Melody Ashton's life. She wished she'd said good-bye.

Back in the sitting room she found no trace of the whole episode, no gory water or stained towels, no decanter, no battered but unbroken nobleman. There was just the faintest scent of brandy and male body—and Mrs. Barstow, clucking like a chicken that's spotted a fox near the henhouse.

"I just brought some fresh hot water, miss, in case you want to freshen up before tea."

Both sounded heavenly, but Melody thought of

her dwindling supply of coins. "Thank you, ma'am, but I didn't order tea, and we agreed not to be a further burden to you. Your giving up your rooms is far more than money alone can repay."

"Nicely spoken, miss. I told that clunch Barstow you were quality. But never you mind. It's all been taken care of by a gentleman whose name I don't recall so don't ask me."

Melody smiled. "You mean the one who wasn't here before?"

"Right. The one I'm to swear on my life you never spent the afternoon with."

"In that case, thank you, tea would be delightful. And please thank the gentleman for me."

"What gentleman might that be?"

"He'll be all right, won't he?"

"No one's ever cocked his toes up in *my* inn, miss. 'Specially not any handsome rogue what's too slippery for the devil to catch."

Nanny woke to the smell of fresh-brewed tea, lemon wafers, and buttered toast fingers with jam.

"You been behaving yourself, missy?"

"I haven't been out of these two rooms, Nanny."

Mrs. Barstow spilled the cream and had to go fetch more.

One night she was dreaming of balls and beaux; the next, fretting over her family's uncertain future. This evening, Melody dreaded blowing out the candle, for fear she would have nightmares of blows landing, bones breaking, blood and bruises and horrid yellow-purple, swollen skin. She didn't. She fell asleep with a smile, and a mind picture of a crooked grin and laughing blue eyes. She hugged the image to herself and never stirred till morning.

Mrs. Barstow brought morning chocolate, hot rolls, and the news that the coach would be out front

33

in an hour. Albert's nephew and two of the grooms
had been working on it since sunup, long before the
bucks were up requiring their services. Melody was
pleased to accept Mrs. Barstow's offer to help her
get ready, saving her scalp from Nanny's ruthless
touch. In forty minutes she was washed, dressed in
a fresh gown, her hair pulled back in a neatly
braided coil, her cape newly sponged and pressed.

When Melody reached for the reticule hanging
off her wrist, Mrs. Barstow was having none of it.
"Reckoning's been paid," she whispered for Melody's ears only. "Nothing improper in that, I made
sure. Just his nibs's way of saying thank you."

Melody waited until Nanny went back to the bedroom to check that they hadn't left anything behind, for the third time. "You've seen him, then?
He's better?"

"Cranky as a crab and uglier nor a pickled pig.
He's down the hall in one of the private parlors
where we moved a cot in to save him the stairs. It
can't be what I'm liking, but he asks if you could
stop in for a minute on your way out."

"It would only be proper to thank him for his
generosity," Melody rationalized. Then Nanny
clomped to her side in heavy boots. "But I don't
think I can."

"That's been taken care of, too, miss." Mrs. Barstow turned to Nanny. "You know, I've been thinking of that mishap of yourn yesterday. A terrible
thing, these ruffians on the road. Anywise, my sister used to be a prodigious needlewoman afore
she moved away. Now her threads and such are in
the attic, likely going to moths, for I never have
time for it, more's the pity. I'd be pleased if you'd
come choose what you could make use of, to make
up for the delay and all."

Mrs. Barstow started Nanny up the stairs, nodding back at Melody toward the first door on the

right. "Ten minutes, miss," she murmured. "And it's against my better judgment. But he's looking as harmless as a babe, so I suppose that's fair."

Melody hesitated outside the door. She really should not do this. Her reputation, her future—his practiced charm. She tapped lightly.

He was sitting, stiffly it seemed to her, in a high-backed chair. He was wearing a bright paisley dressing gown with a black velvet collar and gray pantaloons. The colors of the robe, which was open enough for her to see wide swatches of bandages across his chest, were as nothing compared to the colors of his face.

"Oh my," she said, going closer. "You shouldn't be up."

"And you shouldn't be here."

My word, Corey thought, standing cautiously. He must have taken a harder hit to the brainbox than he thought. Yesterday, with her hair down and her toes bare, his angel was a most appealing little baggage, and he had wanted—needed—just one more look at her dewy innocence to remind him that the world wasn't all hardened cynics. Today she was nothing more than a pretty schoolroom chit, all prunes and prisms, not a hair out of place, bundled sensibly against the cold. By all that was holy, even he had more conscience than to make mice feet of her good name, whatever it was. "You had better leave."

Of course she shouldn't be here. Any peagoose knew that. But hadn't he asked for her and arranged the whole elaborate scheme so she could come? Obviously, he had changed his mind. So had Miss Ashton. Instead of wishing him Godspeed and hoping that by some miracle this nonesuch would ask for her direction, she would stand tall—she had her shoes on today—and make polite inquiries as to his health, then return his largesse. A lady never let a strange man pay her way.

35

She pulled at the strings of her reticule—the weight of the thing was making it devilish hard to undo—and raised her proud chin.

"What the deuce is that thing around your neck?"

Drat Nanny anyway! She couldn't admit the muffler was her own cross to bear, so Melody answered, "It's all the thing, don't you know, my lord." But she showed her adorable dimples, and a lot of the viscount's good resolutions melted.

He raised the one moveable eyebrow. "Perhaps in Shavbrodia, my girl, but in London ladies don't pay attention to the weather. They are wearing the flimsiest of gowns, with the least underpinnings. Some are even dampening their skirts."

Her green eyes opened wide. "They are? Whatever for?"

He grinned. "Child, you have so much to learn. I only wish I . . . No, you had better leave."

"I am not in leading strings, Lord Corey. About your paying my shot at the inn, I do know that's not the thing." She couldn't get the blasted strings unknotted, and the wretched man was laughing at her! She stamped her foot in frustration.

He reached for the bag to help her, and exclaimed, "My God, what's in here? The thing weighs a ton."

She snatched it back, not about to reveal the reticule's contents, but he kept her hand in his, to her confusion. "If you must know, it's a going-away present from my schoolmistress."

"A fine instructor she must be, not teaching her young ladies about the danger of rakes." He was teasing her purposefully, noting her stress on the "going-away" part to distance herself from the schoolroom. He also noticed how the color came and went in her peach-blushed cheeks.

"School taught me everything I need to know, thank you."

36

"Everything, *mon ange*?" With that Corey drew her forward and brushed his other hand across her cheek and behind her head. He lowered his mouth to hers and kissed her, tenderly enough for his bruised lips, thoroughly enough to leave Melody dazed.

Now why the bloody hell had he done that? Corey asked himself. Most likely it was the same devil that had put Albert in his path: he just could not resist a dare. It would never do. The viscount shook himself, bringing his cracked ribs forcibly back to mind.

"Angel, Angel, you mustn't look at me all dewy and awestruck, or I'll forget I am a gentleman altogether. It was only a simple little kiss."

Her first rake. Her first kiss. The first time a second became eternity. And to him it was just a simple kiss? Melody sighed. "I suppose I have a lot to learn, after all."

"You'll get swallowed whole in the ton, else."

"I might never get to London." Never know another libertine, never feel that delicious tingling.

"Well, then your rural society, which can be even more moralistic. I really feel I owe it to you, to finish your education."

Melody felt that his kiss had opened more horizons than all the books in Miss Meadow's library. She sighed again.

His fingers stroked her hand, which was somehow still in his. "The first rule is no sighing; it gives a fellow notions. No, the first rule is never let a man get you off somewhere alone. Then you don't need any other rules. But if you should find yourself alone, say on a starry balcony, and the cur dares to take liberties with you, like this—"

This time the world stopped.

"—then you are supposed to slap him, like this." And he raised her hand to his face, but instead of the slap, her palm caressed his empurpled cheek.

The viscount took a deep, painful breath. "You're not a very apt pupil, are you, sweetheart?" He laughed.

He was laughing at her! "Of all the miserable—"

"That's it, Angel, you are supposed to be mad, not moonstruck. Here, make a fist, since your slaps would not precisely discourage an overheated beau." Corey's hands curled Melody's fingers into a ball, and he grinned at her. "Now pretend I am a randy buck toying with your affections."

She didn't have to pretend. She hauled off and swung at him, she really did. She missed, of course; he ducked back. But her reticule, with its roll of coins and hefty little book, swung right behind her fist—and it didn't miss.

Mingleforth's *Rules of Polite Decorum* came in handy, after all. *Now* Corey's nose was broken.

One other event interrupted Miss Ashton's journey home. Late in the afternoon, a shabby boy ran onto the roadway chasing a small dog, and Toby pulled back on the reins. The pup ran between the sturdy legs of Old Bess and Thimble and stayed there cowering, while the boy shouted louder, and Toby's hearing grew worse.

Nanny positively swelled in anticipation. Now here was someone she could intimidate. Here was a male, dirty, full of profanity, disturbing the right-of-way, and small. He was going to pay for all the indignities she'd suffered at his fellow men's hands. She grabbed the lad by the ear and jabbed him with her knitting needle. She called him a misbegotten whelp and a gorm-grown gallow's bait. She would have gone on for at least an hour, if Melody hadn't taken part.

At first Miss Ashton hadn't even stepped down from the carriage. She was too despondent to care about a foul-mouthed boy and his dog. But it was getting later, and other vehicles might come along, so she intervened. At the sight of a reasonable face, the boy rushed into explanation: "It's me own bloody dog, and the old dungcrow's got no damn business akeepin' me from it. Bloody mutt were worritin' the chickens an' Ma says iffin I catch it, I can help drown the bleedin' bitch."

So Melody slapped the brat. Then she tossed a coin into the dirt at his feet. "There, now it's not your dog any longer. And if you are not out of here in two minutes, I'll send for the magistrate, you little muckworm." The boy grabbed up the coin and ran. Melody used a piece of cheese to coax the dog out from the proximity of Thimble's massive hooves. The little mongrel was ridged-rib starving, shivering, and filthy. It was young, mostly hound with something shaggy mixed in, and it licked Melody's hand in pathetic gratitude. She wrapped it in her wool muffler—with an I-dare-you look to Nanny—and carried it back to the carriage, where the pup had food and water from the hamper before falling asleep in its savior's lap. Melody promptly named her new friend Angel, then proceeded to dampen the poor beast with her tears.

Chapter Six

"*Y*ou brought home another charity case? For heaven's sake, Melody, *we* are a charity case! How could any child of mine be such a skitterwitted ninnyhammer? Where's my hartshorn? I need my salts. Perhaps a cordial."

Lady Jessamyn Ashton was reclining on the lounge in her bedroom, exhausted from the effort of offering her cheek to be kissed. She was interestingly pale, dressed in lavender gauze, and she fluttered a square of silk between her watery eyes and her ample bosom. With an air of die-away frailty, she asked, "Was ever a woman so beset?"

Melody poured out a tonic from the tray nearby. "Come, Mama, things cannot be as bad as all that. You sent me money for new clothes, remember?"

"A lady has to keep up appearances no matter what. Do you think I would let that harpy in Bath discover we are in Dun Territory? The woman has a wider correspondence than I do. Did, alas. I could not bear it if everyone in the ton knew we were below hatches. Could you sprinkle some rosewater on my handkerchief, dear?"

Melody did, and placed it tenderly across her mother's forehead. "But are we?" she persisted. "Are we below hatches?"

Lady Ashton tossed the cloth on the floor, dropping the role of tragedy queen with it. "Don't be such a gudgeon. We've been punting on tick for years. Now there's almost no income at all."

"But, Mama, the way you live, all the clothes and traveling, and my schooling, my allowance. I do not understand."

"Then you are a paperskull, Melody. The only hope we ever had was to find you a wealthy *parti*. The breeding was there, along with a modest dowry, thanks to Judith, and we made sure you had the education the highest sticklers demand in a wife. We encouraged the necessary connections, all those well-born girls at your so-fashionable school, all my so-called friends. Friends, hah! Where are they now, I wonder."

"Do you mean everything was for me to make an advantageous marriage? I thought I was to have a love match."

Lady Jessamyn gave that the consideration it deserved, none. "I researched the prospects for years before settling on Dickie Pendleton, whom I have been cultivating for ages now. He's an earl, and as rich as Croesus, they say, and needing an heir before he's too old to—before much longer at any rate. He wouldn't commit himself till your come out, of course, but we did talk settlements over Christmas at Sally Jersey's."

"Without ... without even asking me?" Melody choked out.

"Of course, the man's the most sanctimonious Methodist in town, and I should have known he'd shab off at the first hint of gossip."

Gossip? Melody's head was already reeling, and

for a moment she wondered if there was talk of her indiscretion—indiscretions—at that inn. Rumor could not possibly have reached Copley-Whitmore, not if Nanny hadn't brought it, and there would have been a rare trimming indeed, in that case. Nothing was making sense! Setting aside the question of Lord Pendleton, forever, she hoped, Melody asked, "What gossip, Mama?"

Lady Jessamyn recalled her persona. She sniffled and dabbed at her eyes. "Ah, if only I knew. Not that it would have mattered either way. With no new money coming in, there isn't enough blunt left for a proper Season: renting a suitable address, throwing a ball, presentation gowns, you know. Mr. Hadley says no one will extend me credit." She pounded her fist on the table. "I should have made the stiff-rumped prig put an offer in writing! No, not Hadley, you twit," Lady Ashton scolded at Melody's gasp. Mr. Hadley was the family's aging man of business. "That twiddlepoop Pendleton. Not that Hadley was any big help. And stop pacing, it is wearing on my delicate nerves."

"Forgive me, Mama, but I just cannot comprehend the situation. We got along for years. What happened? I thought Aunt Judith left us in good stead, and the nabob was always sending money."

"Judith left us the house and its property, your dowry, and all those grubby little mouths to feed. My widow's jointure was barely enough to keep us in candles, without the other income. Then people started talking, invitations were withdrawn, checks stopped coming in."

"What checks were those, Mama? I never knew of any—"

"Didn't they teach you not to interrupt at that fancy place? When the money stopped coming ages ago, I wrote to the nabob, Sir Bartleby, that is, that we found ourselves in temporary embarrassment. Did he even answer? Hah! That's just like a man, underfoot when you least desire them, and least in sight during times of need. Don't tell Felice—the dear child has been such a help to me—but I think her father is not as wealthy as he pretends to be."

What a great match he'd be for Mama then, Melody thought. Out loud, she asked, "So what are we to do now, Mama?"

"Do? Do? How should I know? A lady of my tender sensibilities cannot be expected to deal with financial matters. That's a man's province, child. You'll just have to take it up with Mr. Hadley."

"Me? I mean I? Deal with your man of business?"

"Who else? I told you, you're the only one with any money. Heaven knows Hadley won't let *me* touch that dowry of yours. And dear, do try to do something about those hordes of children, and that dreadful Mr. Pike. Can you pour me out some laudanum before you go? Perhaps I'll write Barty again, after my nap. I'll ring when I need my writing case."

Mr. Pike, the constable? Melody shivered as she started to unpack her belongings, and not just because there was no fire laid in the grate and no maid to carry coals. There seemed to be a lot Mama had not told her, like those checks and the "other income" Lady Ashton glossed over, and rumors, and—ugh—Lord Pendleton. Well, her little chat with Mama relieved one of Melody's worries: she wouldn't be sitting around Copley-Whitmore for the rest of her days, moping over any toplofty aristocrat. No, she'd be trying to straighten out this mingle-mangle, if they did not all land in gaol first.

And then there were the children. Surely, Mama could not have meant that Melody was to take responsibility for the orphans at Dower House; surely, there was some provision for them. Wasn't there?

* * *

Mama's nerves recovered well enough for her to do justice to an excellent luncheon, and the meal encouraged Melody to hope the rest of the doom and gloom was as exaggerated as Lady Ashton's fragile sensitivities. The woman was tough as nails when she chose! The menu included poached salmon, mutton with parsleyed potatoes, tomatoes in aspic, and trifle for dessert. At least they still had Mrs. Tolliver to cook. No pureed peepers or chicken foot soup.

Unfortunately luncheon also included Felice, who would have been even prettier than Melody remembered, with her butter-yellow hair and perfect complexion, if not for the petulant twist to her rosebud mouth and the whine in her high-pitched voice.

"It's about time you got here to pull your weight," she greeted Melody before Lady Jessamyn drifted into the morning room. "I'm no paid servant to be fetching and carrying for your mother, you know. Why should I be concocting tisanes and matching threads, while you are having it soft in some uppity school?"

Melody's training at that same uppity school kept her from inquiring just what Felice was doing there at all. Miss Bartleby had been Aunt Judith's ward, and for as long as Melody could remember she had been bragging about going off to live with her father in India. If she was not going to join the nabob, why wasn't the ungrateful witch seeking a husband, a position or, by Jupiter, a broom? Mama seemed to enjoy her company, however, and the two must have memorized the fashion journals and the *on dits* columns together, judging from the conversation during the meal.

"A lady does not bring unpleasantness to the dining table, my dear." Lady Ashton rejected Melody's pleas to have some of her questions resolved. After luncheon, of course, Mama needed a nap; the strain of her day was so fatiguing. Felice disappeared without a by-your-leave, and Melody went in search of her answers.

Mathematics was not Melody's strong suit; obviously, it was not Mama's either. Lady Ashton's bookkeeping system consisted of a rat's nest of bills, receipts, demand-due notices, and more bills jammed into the pages of an accounts ledger marked Dower House Home for Children.

Melody sat at Aunt Judith's rickety old walnut desk, the dog Angel—now Angie at Mama's dread of the vicar's visit—lying under the desk with her head on Melody's kicked-off slippers. Newly washed and constantly refed, the pup's ribs still looked like a scrub board, and Melody was still her personal deity. "All that wriggling and tail wagging is fine," Melody told the dog, rubbing Angie's head with one bare foot. "But can you add?"

There were slips from mantua-makers and London linen-drapers, jumbled among those from every local merchant in Copley-Whitmore. None were marked paid. The rough sum Melody arrived at in her head was staggering; her addition must be at fault. She turned to the ledger.

On the last marked page, in the credits columns, were sets of initials, dates, and amounts, haphazardly listed in Mama's spidery hand next to the names of children Melody knew to be at Dower House. Heavens, Mama could not be sending the children out to work, could she? Five pounds for Harold. That would be Harry, who never seemed to stay at any of the homes or schools Mama found for him. Perhaps, Melody thought, trying to find some humor in this bumblebroth, Harry had turned thief at the age of twelve and was handing his bounty over to Lady Ashton. Ten pounds, four shillings for Philip. Dear Pip was quite Melody's favorite of the recent Dower House residents, a serious, studious lad of what? He must be all of fourteen by now,

45

unfortunately rendered shy and awkward by a disfiguring port-wine birthmark on one side of his face, which also kept him from attending school, where other lads would make his life a misery. Regrettably, Pip was a natural scholar. The last time Melody was home he had already absorbed all the vicar's teachings and was devouring the library at the Oaks. Maybe Pip was earning his keep by tutoring, but fifty pounds for Ducky?

There was no polite way of putting it; Ducky was a wantwit. His moon face was always smiling and drooling, and he was happy to play with a wooden spoon or a shiny stone or a sunbeam. Nanny doted on him, finally having a baby who would not grow up. No foster parents would ever take him, nor little Meggie, the next entry. Why should anyone pay another ten pounds for a sickly, spindly slip of a thing? For each of Meggie's six winters, Melody recalled, there were fears for the little girl's life, and every minor childhood ailment almost carried her off. No likely family had come forth to adopt the twins yet either, the last entry. Laura and Dora were identical five-year-old imps who resisted all attempts to send them in different directions. Together they were hellions, often talking gibberish that no one understood, except the other twin.

Turning back toward the beginning of the accounts, Melody found many more listings in Aunt Judith's precise script. Some of the names were familiar from her own earlier years, many were not. Various notations indicated dame schools or seminaries. A few were marked His Majesty's Service or Trading Company; most of the latest were simply crossed through in Mama's wavery lines, as though Lady Ashton trembled to do it. Some of the monies cataloged were substantial, many were smaller amounts repeated over years. None of it made sense.

And the blasted dog had chewed up Melody's slippers.

Outside Dower House a sturdy, dark-haired boy was tossing a ball in the air. "What, sent down again, Harry?"

Melody and a chastened Angie had walked down the tree-lined aisle the Oaks was named for and through the home woods toward the smaller building that used to be the estate's dower house, which now was home to the orphans. That is, Melody walked. Angie hop-toed and scampered, woofing at every moving branch and snapping twig.

"I didn't do it, Miss Melody, I swear. Is that your dog? It's a prime 'un, all right. Can I play with it?"

Angie would not go near the boy, until Melody made it clear they were to be friends, at which Angie stole the ball and ran for the woods, to Harry's delight. Harry was chased in turn by an unkempt urchin in a bedraggled pinafore. The other twin had to be somewhere close. And Philip, sitting on the steps, put down the book he was reading to duck his head, take Melody's outstretched hand, and welcome her home, stammering.

"I brought you a book, Pip. McWorly's *Dissertations on Heavenly Bodies* was highly recommended at the academy, although I could not make heads nor tails of it. I'm sure you'll breeze through it, clever lad that you are." She ignored his blushes by kneeling down to the level of the pale little girl sitting next to him, all swaddled from head to toe in Nanny's woolens, with the palest of blonde curls peeking out of her cap. "Hello, Meggie. My, how big you've grown since last summer." For just a moment, as the child smiled at her, she was reminded of Lord Corey. Melody gave herself a mental shake. Only a noddy would see that rake's image in every innocent blond babe. Only a clunch would think of him at all. She went inside.

"Nanny, who pays for the children?" Nanny was feeding Ducky, who only wanted to play with the spoon, filled with porridge or not. Angie scrambled into the kitchen, her hound's nose leading her unerringly through the house to her mistress, or toward food, anyway. Nanny started to grumble when the dog licked up the spills on the floor, on the chair, on Ducky. But Ducky clapped his pudgy hands and grinned, so more food went into his mouth at a faster rate.

"A fine question to be asking, missy. Better you be asking who pays for the clothes on your back and the roof over your head. The children do, that's who. Who did, leastways. Rob Peter to play pool, like always."

"You mean I'm taking food away from the orphans?" Melody gasped at the thought.

"Not you, this rugrat you brought into my kitchen. He's eating the ham I was saving for the children's supper! You ever hear of mince-mutt pie?"

Chapter Seven

$\mathcal{F}$elice insisted on accompanying Melody to Mr. Hadley's office the next morning. "Didn't they teach you anything at that place? A lady can't go traipsing off by herself, you know. Of course, schoolgirls needn't mind their reputations so carefully," she added spitefully, from her two years' advantage, as though no one would be interested in Melody anyway. If the little cat only knew of the interlude in West Fenton with that regular out-and-outer, her rosebud mouth would purse right up with jealousy and freeze that way, like a cod!

Of course, Melody was not about to mention West Fenton. "I don't think one need be so strict in the countryside. After all, I have known everyone hereabouts my entire life." She tied her bonnet strings and pulled on her gloves.

"I'll just walk along with you anyway, to be on the safe side. I'm anxious to hear Mr. Hadley's opinions."

She was most likely anxious to show off her ensemble. Melody was dressed for the early spring morning and the serious nature of her errand. She wore a serviceable blue merino gown with high collar and long sleeves, and a plain chip-straw bonnet. Felice, on the other hand, wore a flimsy short-sleeved, low-necked, Pomona-green striped muslin and a satin bonnet decorated with artificial cherries dangling charmingly just over her brow. The petite blonde tossed a fringed linen square over her shoulders as a sop to the early spring weather. Melody felt sensible, like a drab shopgirl or something.

"But I'll be closeted with Mr. Hadley quite a while, I fear, and you might find the wait tedious." That should take care of any notion Felice had of sitting in on the interview.

"No matter, I have some commissions for Lady Jess in the village."

More bills to run up, Melody assumed dismally. She was hoping Mr. Hadley would explain why they were saddled with such an ungrateful burden, along with everything else. Then she shook herself for being so uncharitable. After all, Felice was as near to an orphan as could be, abandoned among strangers by a father she never knew. Now it seemed he had even reneged on his financial responsibilities. It must be hard on Felice, so used to thinking of herself as a pasha's princess. Besides, living with Mama could not be easy. Just this morning her tea was too cool, her head was too achy to speak with Cook about menus, and her pillows needed turning, twice. Mama kept a little silver bell by her side, and by bedtime last evening Melody was having quite unladylike thoughts about the little chime. This morning Melody had feared she would never be on her way to town. Then she had the happy notion of offering Mama those Minerva Press books.

"What, those rubbishing gothic tales? Perhaps I'll just glance at them, dear, if you and Felice are both quite determined to leave me to my own devices. I cannot read much, naturally, my poor eyes, you know. Were there any of Mrs. Radcliffe's novels?"

Mama was set for the morning.

Melody was wrong; Felice didn't want to come along just to show off her outfit and spend money. She wanted the opportunity to bat her eyelashes and smile coyly at every man they passed. The apothecary's boy out on deliveries was reduced to red-faced sputters; Mr. Highet sweeping in front of his haberdashery made such a low bow he almost tripped off his stoop. Even the spotty young curate tipped his hat and walked right through Mrs. Vicar Elroy's tulip bed. They nodded politely to Miss Ashton as an afterthought, if they noticed her presence at all. Melody felt like a paid companion!

Even Edwin, one of Mr. Hadley's assistants who had been a Dower House boy before going off to school and landing a position, greeted Melody punctiliously before turning to fawn over Felice. He passed Miss Ashton to another underling while begging to be of service to Miss Bartleby. Could he get her a cool drink or a chair, could he help with her errands? And this was the Edwin who used to sneer at Felice for thinking she was better than everyone else. Melody shook her head.

At least Mr. Hadley was happy to see Melody. He patted her hand and told her she was as lovely a young woman as he always knew she would be. Of course, Mr. Hadley was more than sixty, but his sincerity restored a bit of her self-esteem. His views on her current situation, unfortunately, did nothing for her state of mind.

"It's a sad day, my dear. I tried to warn your mother to set money aside, to get beforehand with the world. That's my job, you know, giving advice." He scratched his bald head. "Rainy days always come, you know."

"Just how rainy, er, how bad is the predicament?

51

To tell the truth, Mama's books made as much sense as Euclid."

Mr. Hadley polished his spectacles, not looking her in the eye. "In basic terms, Miss Melody, your mother has just barely outrun the bailiff. She made some poor investments, against my advice, I beg leave to tell you, and then, like many in the fashionable world, continued living above her means. Credit, you know. She was spending on her expectations, but expectations are not money in the bank, when all is said and done."

"That much I gathered from her records. But what I do not understand is what expectations Mama had. If not an inheritance from Aunt Judith, or settlements from my father, how had she hoped to afford to live the way she was? No one will tell me."

"The contributions, of course."

"You mean the money donated for the orphans?" Melody had a very uncomfortable feeling in the pit of her stomach.

"Oh dear, I thought you knew by now. You see, it started with your Aunt Judith, Miss Morley. She was a spinster lady, you will recall, with no family to speak of except your mother, who was at the time recently married to your father and living in London. Judith had the Oaks with its few acres, and a small competence, and was already responsible for Sir Bartleby's daughter."

"Felice."

"Ahem. Sir Bartleby's support included provision for your aunt, naturally, which enabled her to take in another unfortunate, ah, child. Your mother in London, meanwhile, met various ladies who, ah, wished to see such children given a better life than foundling hospitals offered. So, they became sponsors in the new Dower House Home for Children."

"Do you mean they made charitable gifts?"

"It was more than that. To sponsor a child, a

patron had to pledge to provide for that particular boy or girl through infancy and onward, right up to getting them started in a career or dowered to a respectable marriage. Other times the sums were provided to help the foster parents your Aunt Judith found, families who otherwise could not afford another mouth to feed."

"How kind of those ladies to make such a commitment."

Mr. Hadley took out a handkerchief and dabbed at this brow. "Ah, indeed. I helped draw up some of the papers myself. Now some of the sponsors chose to pay—ah, make their donations—monthly or yearly. Others made one large deposit to the Dower House account. Here is where it gets a bit ticklish."

That nasty feeling in Melody's stomach was arguing with her breakfast. Aunt Judith was a rigid moralist, who would never have touched the orphans' money. Mama could *not* have, could she? Melody was certain Mr. Hadley did not mean ticklish as in funny, but she had to ask. "How?"

"You see, it was understood with each contribution that your aunt, then your mother, was to have a share of the financial benefits, for their efforts and attention to the children. When there was a lump sum, an endowment if you will, the interest would accrue to Lady Morley, for her expenses in operating the home, et cetera. Then your father died and left all of those debts, and you and your mother came to live with Lady Morley. Slightly more of the, ah, principles were withdrawn. With Lady Morley's passing, I am afraid your mother became a tad careless with her bookkeeping."

"As in which was the orphans' money and which was hers?"

"Something like that. She did feel that by investing the principles she could increase the, ah, profits. As I said, the investments failed. All would still have been well, however, if she had stopped spending, or if the, ah, gifts continued coming."

"But?" It was strange. Mr. Hadley kept mopping at his forehead as if he were overwarm, while Melody was chilled through.

"But recently the money has not kept coming. Your mother feels this may be due to certain rumors circulating in the ton."

"She mentioned the same to me. Do you have any idea what these stories are about?"

"I do not travel in those circles, of course. If I had to guess, my dear, I'm afraid I would have to say that people think your mother is stealing from the children."

There, it was said. Melody had refused to put the idea into words, although the notion had niggled at the back of her mind since seeing that ledger. Now she refused to believe it. "No," she firmly declared. "Not my mother. Mama is a lady."

Isn't she? a tiny voice asked. Melody overruled it and stiffened her already straight back in the hard chair. "We'll come about, you'll see. Mama mentioned that the dowry you hold for me, as trustee, could see us through this temporary setback, so I must ask you to release those monies to me."

"But, my dear, how will you contract a marriage, then?"

"I am afraid I am not likely to encounter eligible gentlemen in debtors' prison either, Mr. Hadley."

"But you are only seventeen, child. Your whole future lies ahead. You won't want to forfeit it now. Perhaps one of your schoolmates could invite you to town for the Season."

"What, shall I go off to enjoy myself, turning my back on my family and my responsibilities?"

The old man shook his head. Her mother surely would. "I cannot let you do this, my dear, but I respect your valiant sacrifice."

"Thank you for your concern, Mr. Hadley, but

54

what kind of future would I have if I could not respect myself?"

They compromised. Mr. Hadley would let Melody have half of the money Aunt Judith had put aside for her, if it stayed in her own hands. The chit had bottom, he acknowledged, and a sensible mind that wouldn't be sidetracked by fancy frills and furbelows. There was a lot more of Judith Morley in the lass than she knew. If anyone could get that house in order—and Dower House, too—young Melody was it. Too bad such weight had to fall on such tender shoulders. At least Mr. Hadley felt he could relieve her of one burden.

"Don't you go thinking that Miss Felice is another of your responsibilities. Judith provided for her, too, but the chit went through the blunt in one year, and some of those other monies we talked of, trying to nab herself a title, tagging along with your mother to those house parties and such. If ever there was a wench with ideas above her station it's that one."

"I thought the nabob, Sir Bartleby, was to send for her."

"We all did, but he hasn't been heard from. I thought for a while she'd make a match with young Edwin, but he wasn't good enough for her, nor were any of the local lads. She has her heart set on a London swell, it seems."

"She's very beautiful."

"And pretty is as pretty does, I don't need to remind you. Besides, what fancy gent is going to offer for a dowerless chit who cannot even dance at Almack's?" Mr. Hadley tidied the papers on his desk, pleased that the issue of Felice was dispensed with. He'd lost too many hours of work with Edwin's mooning after the heartless jade.

"But why wouldn't Felice get her vouchers?" Melody asked, confused. "I always thought Sir Bartleby was of the highest stare."

55

"That's because you listened to Miss Bartleby, I'll warrant. He only got knighted after years with the East India Company, you know, for lending so much of the ready to the crown. Bartleby wasn't married before he left the country either, and he left under some kind of cloud. You might say Felice was the silver lining."

Then again, you might say Felice was the dark shadow on a sunny day. Here Melody had her head full of important ideas: which bills to pay first, where they could best economize, how she could earn a living and see to the others at the same time. And there was Felice, grousing because Mrs. Finsterer would not let her put the purchase of a pair of York tan gloves on Lady Ashton's account.

"Can you believe the nerve? These provincial shopkeepers should be pleased to do trade with us."

"They would be more pleased to be paid what's owed them," Melody replied, sharper than she intended. Some of the other merchants must have been more lenient than Mrs. Finsterer, or more optimistic, or males, since Felice had a whole pile of packages. She was quick to transfer the bundles to Melody's arms, while retying her bonnet strings, and somehow that's where the parcels stayed.

"Oh, but now that you have settled with Mr. Hadley," Felice chirped, turning her brightest smile on Melody, "you can go back and reestablish our credit."

"I'm sorry," Melody told her, "but there will be no more credit." Truthfully, she wasn't sorry a bit. She wasn't even sorry when the sun went behind a cloud, and the underdressed, pouting, little blond tart shivered the whole way home.

Chapter Eight

*M*elody was going to make this work. She had to; there was no other choice. So what if she knew nothing about holding household or raising children? She didn't know anything about pigs and chickens and turnips, either, and that was not going to stop her. She would just have to learn, she told herself with uncrushed youth's cheerful belief in invincibility, and the others would have to learn with her.

She made lists and talked to more knowledgeable persons: old Toby, Mr. Hadley, the neighboring landlord's bailiff, even a poacher brought to the house one dark evening by Mrs. Tolliver, the cook, to show Melody how to lay snares. And she enlisted the children, who were thrilled to help until their hands got blisters turning over a vegetable patch. Still, if the Morley-Ashton households were to become self-sufficient, everyone had a job to do.

Sturdy Harry was the biggest assistance, although he kept trying to convince Melody their best bet was to start a racing stable.

"I know you are horse mad, Harry, but hogs are cheaper to buy, less costly to feed, grow faster, and we can eat them."

"I know horses are expensive, but think of all the money left over from my schooling. That last place won't have me back, you know," he told her, grinning. "And the fire wasn't even my fault."

Philip volunteered his services as a tutor, to Harry's disgust, and to teach the younger children their letters, to save money there. "I—I'm not real strong like Harry, Miss Melody, b-but I am awfully good with figures. P-perhaps, that is, if you want, I could help with the b-books."

Now there was a welcome offer! After studying the accounts with Melody after dinner that very night, Pip even found a way to save money by paying the bills off in part, leaving some of their funds earning interest. "B-because the merchants will be pl-pl—happy to get any of what's due, and they'll see you mean to make good."

"I knew you were a downy one, Pip! Of course, I'll need you with me to explain it to them," she mentioned casually, starting another of her campaigns. Before he could object she went on: "I don't think I have the same grasp of finances you do. I'd only make a mull of it, you know."

Pip handsomely conceded that females weren't expected to understand such weighty matters, and yes, she ought to have a man, or a boy, at her side.

The twins, who were always filthy despite Nanny's best efforts, were naturally put in charge of the new pigs, once the pen was built. Then delicate Meggie, wrapped like a mummy in Nanny's knitteds, wanted a job all her own. She got the chickens and handled those eggs like fragile porcelain.

Ducky learned to weed, more or less, under Nanny's supervision. More weeds and less cabbage and parsley seedlings, thank goodness, Melody cheered. And Nanny, of course, kept her needles flying. With all the new wool, she declared, they wouldn't go cold for another three years. They might even try selling mittens in the village, come next winter.

Melody was determined that even the pup, Angie, would earn her keep. There were rabbits and partridge and pheasants in the home woods that could be better utilized on the home dinner table. Angie could scent food miles away—she was already *canis non grata* in the village—so all Melody had to do was convince the dog to help her locate supper in the wild. Of course, after Angie flushed the game, Melody had to shoot it, which posed a few obstacles of its own, considering Melody had never handled a gun in her life. She would learn.

Two other obstacles were not as easily overcome: Mama and Felice.

"My dearest daughter out there in the muck with pigs and chickens? My salts, quickly."

It got worse when Melody determined that the most money could be saved by combining the two households.

"Don't be a ninnyhammer, Melody. You cannot expect me to permit those, those *children* to come live at the Oaks, can you?"

"No, Mama, I expect you to go live at the Dower House."

"Oh, dear Lord, my heart. I'm having spasms, you sapskull, call the physician."

"Mama, we cannot afford to heat this pile, much less pay enough staff to keep it clean. The idea of an army of servants waiting on three women is absurd anyway, even if we had the means."

Tears did not work either, nor cajolery, nor guilt. "You are an unnatural child, trying to kill your own mother. I am not a well woman, you know. Living at the Dower House with the children, all the noise and *dirt* . . . I'm afraid it will be too much for me."

Melody wasn't budging, and she held the purse strings. She also hid that little silver bell.

"Don't give me that perishing cordial, you nod-cock, I need the brandy."

"I am sorry, Felice, but we cannot afford a dresser for you and Mama. In fact, the few servants we do keep will be too busy, so you'll have to look after my mother, help with her clothes and things."

Felice turned another page of the fashion magazine. "You cannot make a maid out of me, Miss High-and-Mighty. I won't do it."

"Then you won't eat."

Felice threw the magazine down and stamped on it. "My father shall hear of this!"

"Good, I'd like to have a few words with that gentleman myself. Perhaps he can advise me on some investments, if he ever reimburses the money spent on your behalf. Shall I show you the tally Pip made of that last stack of bills?" The beauty made no reply. "*Three* parasols, Felice?"

"I wouldn't expect a dowd like you to understand. They were for three different outfits, of course."

"But I do understand, Felice, and I sincerely hope you bought quality merchandise, for it will have to last you a good long time."

"You always were hateful, Melody Ashton, you with your so-perfect manners and your so-dignified airs. Well, you don't fool me for a minute; you're just jealous. You'll never get a husband, and you want to make sure I never get one! Why, even that windbag Lord Pendleton wouldn't have a managing female like you!"

Melody's innate honesty forced her to admit to the germ of truth hidden in the vitriol. Not that claptrap about husbands, of course, but the charge of jealousy hit home. All the attention Mama gave the other girl, all the stares from all the men, for all those years, hurt. Still, she could be fair. "You would be beautiful dressed in rags, Felice, and gentlemen will continue to offer for you, I am sure. Please believe me, I shall heartily wish you joy with whichever man you accept . . . the sooner the better."

They planted potatoes and fenced in the chickens. The merchants were cooperating, and the two sows gave birth. Unfortunately, piglets could fit through gaps their lumbering mothers could not.

"Pigs like to wander," Toby informed Melody. So wires were strung.

"Pigs can dig." So boards were sunk.

Pigs could chew, and pigs could jump. Pigs could fly, for all Melody knew, and likely would before she found a way to keep them penned. So there were always little pink piglets in the garden, on the lawn, or down the drive, and almost always two identically dirty little girls chasing after them. Sometimes the boys joined in, and sometimes Angie, adding her baying to the giggling, shouting, squealing melee. They seemed to save the best, noisiest, muddiest pighunts for when Lady Ashton was taking her constitutional or when the vicar came to call. No one even bothered to hand Lady Jessamyn her smelling salts anymore; they went straight for the brandy.

Melody was practicing her shooting, using her father's old dueling pistol that Toby had taught her how to load and aim. The gun would be no good over distance, but in her careful reasoning, Melody felt she would do better to start with a stationary target at short range. Frankly, she wasn't sure she could shoot a bunny rabbit. There was a certain amount of pleasure, meanwhile, in the skill she was gaining.

She was concentrating on the day's target, a playing card, and never heard the man approaching till Angie's bark grew sharper.

" 'Ere, 'ere, call your dog off, miss."

"It's Mr. Pike, the constable, isn't it? How do you do, sir?"

Pike removed his low-crowned hat and bowed, revealing a rat-brown wig slightly askew on his head. "Aye, miss. They said as how you were the one I had to talk to, concerning the complaints."

"What complaints might those be, sir?" Melody asked, reloading the pistol.

"Well, ma'am, there's complaints from the shop-keepers about bills, complaints from the butcher about your dog, and complaints from the villagers about the bast—brats."

"Oh, those complaints." The man obviously had no sense of humor. He merely wiped at his pointed red nose, where another drip was already forming. "Yes, well, I believe I have accommodated the merchants, and Angie here has not repeated her foray to the village."

"And what about the youngsters? There's some as saying they belong in the workhouse."

"That's absurd." She looked at him narrowly. "Unless 'they' get a portion of the county dole for each resident there. Those children are my responsibility, not to be thrown on the parish."

"But law-abiding citizens are saying they're running around wild and unsupervised, and you're keeping freaks out here."

Melody drew herself up and looked down on the little man—they always were small, bullies like this. "Mr. Pike, those are lovely, happy children you are speaking of. They are well fed, properly clothed, and have lessons every day. I'll thank you not to call them names. Now if you are finished, sir, I have more practicing to do."

Pike rubbed his hands together. "You haven't answered all of the charges, miss." He edged a little closer, looking at her sideways. "Of course, I'd forget some of the complaints if you were to make it worth my while. A little snuggling might do it."

"Sir, you forget yourself!"

"No, I remember Miss Felice used to cooperate."

Why, that little yellow-haired baggage! Melody turned away and pointed the gun. "Mr. Pike, I am going to forget this conversation." She aimed at the card. "I suggest you do the same." And fired. She hit the card, the knave of spades, right on the nose. "Do I make myself clear?"

It was time to try Papa's rifle.

They harvested the first row of beans, sold some of the farrow pigs, thankfully before the twins could count, and Melody shot her first woodcock. Of course, she had to wrestle with Angie over possession of the bird, but she was working on the problem. Felice was spending more time in the village, fixing her interest on Edwin, Melody hoped, and Mama was resting, if not resigned. They were managing. Mr. Hadley told Melody she should be proud.

At night sometimes, though, when her body was exhausted but her mind was wide awake, and she only had Angie for company, Miss Ashton stared at the ceiling of her tiny room and despaired.

Should a person stop dreaming because no dreams have come true? Stop wishing when no wishes are fulfilled? Then where is the place for heaven? How can life itself go on without hope? It cannot; that's called hell. At the very least, one can hope for a sunny day or an end to rain. Small dreams, but fair odds, sooner or later.

And a young girl, even one with freckles from working out in the sun, should never give up her dreams. Sooner or later . . .

Chapter Nine

*S*ooner or later, a man has to pick up the threads of his life, even if his nose *is* crooked. Lord Cordell Inscoe, Viscount Coe, had stayed away from London for over a month. The first few weeks, of course, were not by choice.

"You take that deathtrap vehicle out of the carriage house, and I won't be responsible," the doctor announced when he came to the inn to do what he could for the viscount's nose. "One rut, one miscue to those fractious brutes you young blades drive, and one of those cracked ribs goes right through your lung. Then where are you? Lying in a road somewhere, gasping for air like a beached perch. And what did you say happened to your nose, anyway? You fell? Addlepated young fool, I told you to keep quiet. Lucky you didn't do yourself an injury right here, in Mrs. Barstow's best parlor."

Lucky? If the cantankerous old sawbones thought a broken nose was no injury, he should just get a taste of what it felt like. Coe had a mind to—

"Too bad I couldn't get here yesterday when it

happened. Mrs. Reilly, don't you know. For real this time, by Jupiter, great big bruiser of a boy, it was. Already set a bit, your beak, that is. I'll have to break it again, of course, unless you want to be sniffing at your right ear the rest of your days. This might pain you some."

If Corey didn't flatten the physician right then, it was because he was too busy picturing a slim, graceful neck between his hands.

So he stayed on in West Fenton for his ribs' sake, not eager for anyone to see him in his present condition anyway. Hostesses would faint, the fellows at the clubs would be merciless in their ribbing, without even knowing about the little girl who'd dealt the last blow, and his town house staff would wrap him in cotton wool. Corey thought for a moment of lying low as soon as he could travel to the little house in Kensington he kept for his convenients. He was not paying his current mistress Yvette for her conversation, however, and not being up to the obvious exercise, he might as well stay put..

Corey sent for his man Bates, his ex-batman from army days, now a dapper gentleman's gentleman, who took his stature from serving a pink of the ton. Lord Coe also notified his secretary to refuse invitations, forward important mail, and handle everything else. The viscount's affairs were well in hand, as they had to be, with him gone so long fighting old Boney. He trusted his bailiffs and his bankers and Mr. Tyler, who had been secretary to his father before him.

The first week Corey took laudanum for the pain; the second, Bates was hiding his master's boots to keep the viscount from overdoing. By the third week Coe was visiting Albert, playing cards in the taproom with the worshipful locals, and making a nuisance of himself in the stables, wanting to exercise the horses. Mostly, he went for walks and reflected on his life. Time and boredom will do that to a man.

The war was over, his part of it anyway, and maybe he *was* taking too many risks with his life. Maybe he should think about leaving more to posterity than a new driving record to Brighton. The viscountcy was secure, at least, in a sober cousin and his large, hopeful brood. Coe's personal wealth, the considerable unentailed property, would go to his beloved sister and her future children. Erica, Lady Wooster, was now a childless widow living in Bath, but she was only twenty-four, and that could change. Now that Corey had time to think about it, his heritage demanded more of him. He would just have to change his way of life—or find Erica a new husband.

London was a little thin of company when he finally got there, the Season not formally underway. The clubs seemed to have the same gouty gents sitting under a pall of smoke, the same glitter-eyed gamblers feverishly dicing away their patrimonies, and the same hard-edged tulips shredding reputations over cognac. The parks were full of dandies on the strut and hey-go-mad bucks on bonecrushers. Erica's first marriage was a joyless one, Corey thought regretfully, still feeling guilty for his part in arranging it. She deserved better.

With this thought in mind, or so he told himself, Viscount Coe went to Almack's. The beau monde's Marriage Mart worked both ways, he reasoned, and a gentleman on the lookout to become a tenant for life would more likely be found here than at, say, the Coconut Club or the Cyprian's Ball. If, while he reconnoitered the field of bachelors, the viscount's eye happened to glance to the rows of white lace decked debutantes, that was merely by accident.

As Lord Coe temporized for a stunned Lady Jersey, he was just popping by in case an old friend was up from the country. The elusive, reckless Lord Coe at Almack's surveying this year's crop of fledglings? What a tale to pass around! Reading her mind, Corey tugged at his neckcloth, an elegant creation it had taken him and Bates an hour to tie. It may be de rigueur to arrive at Almack's before eleven, and in knee smalls at that, and even to flirt with Lady Jersey, but dashed if he'd let the lady patronesses pass him off to every whey-faced chit and her eager mama. He was not about to give rise to hopeful expectations in any grasping woman's breast.

He had one dance with Princess Esterhazy before excusing himself. "I see that my, ah, friend is not here, so I'll just be going on. Another engagement, don't you know."

That wouldn't stop the rumors, not when his lordship kept scanning the sidelines.

She wasn't there, his green-eyed sprite, not that he would admit looking for her. She said she would not have a Season, but such a beauty deserved gowns and jewels and elegant waltzes—in his arms. After he strangled her, of course. He touched the bridge of his nose where there was and might always be a new bump, and smiled, causing one dumpling of a deb to nearly swoon with joy. The viscount did not notice.

This was absurd, he chided himself, looking for Angel amid such milk-and-water misses! Looking for her at all was foolish beyond permission. That's why he had purposely not asked Barstow for her direction, debating with himself whether Mrs. Barstow would have given it. Why, his behavior toward an untouched maiden was already reprehensible, and he was no closer to jumping into parson's mousetrap over a pair of green eyes and a captivating dimple than he was to . . . to asking that plump little chit over there for a dance. The wealthiest, most attractive, most alluring bachelor in many a year scowled and stomped out of Almack's. Miss Weathersfield fled in tears to the retiring room, while all the young sprigs of fashion wondered how they could get such interesting deviations in their proboscises.

At least Yvette could not be tarnished by his rake-shame reputation, Coe thought as he walked off his ill-humor on the long trek to Kensington. Hell, she'd helped him earn it, along with many of her sisters. Now it was time she earned that charming little bijou and the pony cart and the diamond necklace.

Yvette earned the matching bracelet, leaving Corey spent. Too bad she could not satisfy his mind as well as his body, but Yvette's talents did not include beguiling conversation. There was no friendly banter, no natural tenderness, or warm good humor. For the first time ever, Coe was bothered by bought affection. He went home early.

A few tedious weeks later, the best Viscount Coe had managed for entertainment was a green-eyed replacement for Yvette, some heavy wagers, and the idea of a house party at his property outside Bath, to liven up his sister's days. The best prospect he could come up with for a new brother-in-law was Lord Pendleton, and even Corey was hesitant about foisting the prosy bore on Erica for a fortnight. Then Erica wrote him a troubled letter, asking if he could help with a delicate matter. Her words spoke of adventure, danger, and intrigue, a menace to his dear sister's happiness, and a threat to the family name. What could be better?

It rained for four days. The viscount put up at Hazelton, a town about an hour from his goal, according to his maps. He had decided to keep this distance, not wanting his destination made public. He knew what a stir a nobleman and his retinue could make in a small village, which was precisely what he wished to avoid in such a delicate family matter. He could not simply travel by horseback, for he needed the closed carriage, which meant a coachman, footmen, and postilions. A groom was necessary to look after his stallion, Caesar, tied behind. The viscount's man, Bates, refused to be left behind, saying: "Just look what happened last time, milord." So Hazelton it was.

It kept raining, however, and the only inn in town was damp. Corey's ribs ached, damn the quack in West Fenton. His man, Bates, came down with a cold, and the groom reported one of the carriage horses was off its feed. Blast this whole mission!

He set out finally on a high-strung gray stallion that hadn't been exercised in too long a time, down muddy roadways and up mired country lanes. He got lost twice and almost unseated once, to the detriment of his temper. At last he spotted a gravel drive, as per his directions, flanked by two stone columns with acorns carved in them. Original, he thought sarcastically, prepared to find nothing pleasing about this place. He was not disappointed.

The drive was rutted and weed choked under a canopy of ancient oaks. Last year's leaves formed a slippery roadbed of muck in places, and this year's leaves dripped water off Coe's beaver hat and down his collar. He hated it.

Caesar, meanwhile, hated sudden noises and small, darting creatures. So when the pig jumped out from the underbrush, and the grubby child darted after it inches from the huge stallion's nose, Lord Coe suddenly found himself seated in that same leaf-mold sludge. Corey held his breath and checked his ribs, while high-pitched voices chattered out of sight like monkeys in trees, for all the words he could distinguish. Only Lord Coe's dignity was injured, which the back of his fawn trousers would advertise nicely, thank you. Well, he wasn't turning back. He remounted and kept Caesar on a

69

much tighter rein, swearing the benighted horse was laughing at him.

The drive ended, at last, at a large stone house set in an untended clearing. The windows were grimy, the steps hadn't been swept, and no one came to hold his horse.

"Hallo, the house!" he called, notifying the butler to send one of his minions. No one came. Corey could not very well leave Caesar standing untended, not with misplaced children and livestock popping up anywhere. "Hell and damnation."

"I say, sir, would you like me to hold your horse?"

Corey saw two boys dash toward the house. The speaker, a dark-haired, ruddy-faced lad with his knees muddied and his shirt untucked, was already fearlessly rubbing Caesar's nose. "He's a prime goer, I'll bet," the boy said, adding on another hurried breath, "I'm Harry, that's Pip." The other, sandy-haired lad, ducked his head and stood behind his companion.

Dismounting, Corey reluctantly handed the reins into Harry's eager, but grimy, hands. "You're not the groom here, are you?" he asked. No gentleman would let such a ragamuffin near his cattle.

"Oh no, sir," Harry replied, never taking his eyes off the stallion, "I'm one of the ba—"

Pip kicked him and came forward, eyes still on the ground. "We're b-boys from D-Dower House, sir." He nodded in the direction of a side path, inadvertently showing the splotched side of his face. Corey inhaled deeply, but his expression did not change from a grim, disapproving glower.

Just then the child with the pig came tearing around the building and down a path, pigtails flying, petticoats dragging in the mud, tongue running on wheels.

"What is she, a red Indian, or something?" Corey asked Harry, who seemed to have Caesar under perfect control, despite the screeching whirlwind.

It was Pip—what kind of name was Pip?—who answered: "She ... she's Czechoslovakian, sir." He turned his back on Corey.

That didn't sound like Czech to Coe, from his days of fighting with the allies, but before he could pursue the thought, Harry shouted out: "Hey you, you better get home and out of those dirty clothes before Miss Mel catches you. She'll take a stick to you, else."

Corey could not believe the manners of these boys. " 'Hey you' ?"

Harry wasn't fazed. "Don't know her name," was all he said, bending to find some fresh grass for Caesar. In fact, Harry didn't even seem to notice he was addressing a gentleman, much less a peer of the realm. For the first time in his life, Lord Coe's horse was getting more respect than he was!

The ramshackle place was even worse than Corey had expected. The children were unmannered, untaught, unwashed—and beaten, if Harry could be believed. The viscount marched determinedly up the path to the house, to be nearly bowled over by the same knee-high dust devil. He looked back at Harry, who merely shrugged as if to say, 'Women.'

No one answered the door, not even when Corey banged the knocker and shouted. The damned manor was locked up and deserted! He strode back down the path to look accusingly at the boys.

"Oh," Harry said, noting with surprise the viscount's irritation. "You didn't ask. They're all at Dower House. This place is for rent. Jupiter, you're not here to look it over, are you? By all that's holy, that would be famous! There's a bang-up stable that just needs some work, and I could—"

"Hold, bantling. I am here to see Lady Ashton, not lease her house." Corey noted Harry's crestfallen expression and added, "But you may walk Caesar here if your friend would be so good as to show me the way to the Dower House." There was no reason to take his anger at the situation out on the children. After all, they were the real victims. He softened his tone toward the other boy: "Pet names are fine for the nursery, but between men I think proper names are more fitting, don't you? I am Cordell Coe."

Pip brightened instantly, forgetting to look down. "Oh, indeed, sir. I'm Philip. Philip M-Morley, that is."

"I am pleased to make your acquaintance, Master Philip. Perhaps you could tell me—"

Philip could not tell him anything. He was rooted on the walkway, his mouth hanging open in horror. Corey followed his gaze down the trail and almost choked. The tiny swineherdess had listened to Harry after all, about taking her clothes off and washing up. There she was, giggling on the path, as pink and shiny as one of her pigs—and just as bare.

Pip wanted to die. Whatever must this fine gentleman think? There was no doubt Mr. Coe was a gentleman, maybe even a lord. Zeus, maybe Pip should have been calling him 'my lord.' "M-M—Sir, th-th . . ." Pip just couldn't get it out.

Corey had turned his back on the little nymph, not so much from a sense of honor as an effort to hide his smile from the mortified boy. Somehow there she was, behind them now on the path, still as naked as a jay. The viscount turned his back again, then once more, before finally giving in to delighted chuckles. So there were two of the hell babes. Gads, how they would terrorize the countryside! When he could stop laughing, he patted Philip on the back in a comradely gesture. "Don't worry, old chap, I had a little sister, too." Of course, Corey's sister would never have shown even her ankle in public, and would have been on bread and water for days if she did.

Pip was comforted, nonetheless, and relaxed

enough to say, "Things are usually not this b-bad. Miss Ashton's out hunting, that's all."

So the person supposed to be supervising these waifs was enjoying herself riding to hounds. Corey had a few choice words to say to that harpy, along with his speech for the blood-sucking mother. In the meantime, this place was better than a farce. His ill-humor was in abeyance, and he was actually looking forward to whatever came next. Pigs, bare-bottomed moppets, abandoned houses, what could follow? Dancing cows and two-headed chickens?

The viscount was prepared for almost anything—except Felice.

Chapter Ten

$\mathcal{T}$he door opened at his knock, for a surprise. Corey expected a manservant or at least a maid, not the petite vision throwing him a pert curtsy. She was spring, in a daffodil-yellow gown with grass-green ribbon streamers tied just under full, rounded breasts. A tiny green cap nestled among curls the color of buttercups, and eyes like April mornings twinkled up at him over a rosebud mouth. Viscount Coe could feel the sap rising.

Philip scuffled his feet in disgust. This stranger was no nonpareil after all; he was just like every other moonstruck clodpole in the neighborhood. His mouth was gaping, and he was more tongue-tied than Pip at his worst. Over Felice! Hero-worship died aborning.

"I-I'll just go help Harry with the horse," the boy said, backing down the path and shaking his head. Wait till he told Harry what a looby the paragon turned out to be.

Pip's words broke the spell, and Viscount Coe recalled he was a man of the world, not a green schoolboy. Besides which, he was here on a mission. Business before pleasure, he pledged himself, but what a pleasure it would be. Corey withdrew one of his cards and turned down a corner to show he called in person. "I would like to see Lady Jessamyn Ashton, please."

Felice read the card. A viscount, delivered right to her door! And not just any titled nobleman, but one the *on dits* columns credited with great wealth and great success with the ladies. Felice did not need any stale London dailies to tell her why. The square chin, broad shoulders, and devilishly handsome grin told enough of the story. Now Felice merely had to rewrite the ending, which always termed Coe a perpetual bachelor. Not if she could help it!

"Won't you come sit down?" she offered, taking his riding crop and hat, and leading the way to a sitting room. Courtesy made him follow; the view from the back made him smile appreciatively. "You must be wondering where all the servants are. I don't usually answer the door myself, you know." She gave a tinkling little laugh, looking around for a likely spot to lay his things, as though she never had to worry about such mundane chores. "They are all . . . all given the day off. Yes, that's it. Lady Ashton is so generous, you know. There was a . . . a wedding in the village today." There, now her circumstances wouldn't look so no-account, and she'd even dropped a hint about weddings!

"I am sorry to bother you at a time when things are all at sixes and sevens, then," he replied politely. "And no, I shan't sit in all my dirt." Corey could just imagine this china doll's reaction to muddy stains from the back of his pants. He underestimated Miss Bartleby.

"Oh, we're quite informal here, my lord." She waved a tiny white hand around. The room *was* shabby, with bits and pieces of ribbons, colored

75

chalks, and picture books everywhere. Felice realized just how shabby and quickly disassociated herself from such pedestrian surroundings. "Oh la, what you must think. These are temporary quarters only, don't you know, while the Great House"—that sounded better than the Oaks—"is undergoing refurbishing. The noise and the dirt would be too much for dear Lady Jessamyn."

If Felice meant to suggest her own delicate sensibilities, she missed the mark, for Corey's eyes were not quite so dazzled here in better light, where that fresh blush on the beauty's cheeks appeared a trifle too regular. The trance was wearing thin, under a chiming laugh that was beginning to grate on his nerves like a dinner gong reverberating too long. The boys had said the mansion was for let, not under reconstruction, and if any army of servants had been next or nigh either place for months, he'd eat his hat. Furthermore, who the hell was this pocket Venus, and what was she doing here?

"If you could just give Lady Ashton my card, Miss—?"

"Oh dear, how silly of me! I am Felice Bartleby, Lady Ashton's ward. Actually, I was her sister Judith Morley's ward, and now that I am grown I suppose I no longer fit that description. Perhaps you have heard of my father, Sir Bostwick Bartleby? No? He is quite well known in the Crown Colonies. As soon as he returns we shall be setting up household in London. Mayfair, of course. I'll be sure to put your name on our list for balls and such." His lordship did not take up that gambit, so Felice hurried on: "My, you must think me a sad rattle. It's just so delightful to find a kindred spirit here in the wilds. I'll take your card right on up to Lady Ashton and see if I cannot find where that naughty butler of ours hides the refreshments a gentleman like yourself appreciates." She curtsied daintily and minced out of the room, where she raced down the hall, viciously kicked a ragdoll out of her way, and took the stairs two at a time.

"How many times do I have to tell you, Melody, my nerves—Oh, it's you, Felice." Lady Ashton stopped trying to hide the flask in the bedclothes. Since it was not yet noon, Lady Ashton was not yet risen. "I thought you were walking to the village to see if the new fashion journals had arrived."

"Yes, but we have a caller. You have to get up and come talk to him. Wait till you see those shoulders. Weston made the jacket, of course. He's divine."

Lady Ashton was studying the card. "Inscoe, Inscoe," she ruminated, tapping the card on her teeth. Jessamyn Ashton knew her Debrett's better than her Bible, and it took only seconds for her to place Lord Coe's family. She threw the card from her as if something with ten legs were climbing across it. "Is the constable with him?"

"No, he's by himself, and so exquisite. Do hurry!"

"Thank heavens he hasn't brought the magistrate down on us. Yet." She burrowed under the covers. "I won't see him."

"You *have* to see him. Otherwise he might go away!" Felice ruthlessly pulled back the sheets.

"Stop that, you ninny. He won't go anywhere. He's Erica Wooster's brother."

"He doesn't seem at all toplofty, and with his reputation he cannot be so particular."

"His reputation ain't to the point, and it's no worse than that of any other handsome and hot-blooded young buck on the town for a few years. These young rakeshames think all is well and good when their own pleasure is at stake, but let there be a hint of scandal near their womenfolk or their fine old family names, and there is hell to pay. No, I won't see any niffy-naffy lordling with his dander up."

"But what shall I tell him?" Felice wailed.

"Tell him . . . tell him I am too ill to leave my couch; he has to see Melody. What's that you're doing with the decanters? You're not taking the good stuff? Oh, my heart, a pain right here . . ."

Felice tripped back into the sitting room with a hastily assembled tray of Lady Ashton's finest alongside the children's luncheon dessert. She again urged the viscount to sit and take refreshment, for Lady Jessamyn was indisposed, and Miss Ashton was out and about.

"I thought she was on a foxhunt."

A foxhunt, when they hadn't kept more than a dray pony in years? Felice thought furiously, frantic to disinterest him in Melody before that marplot reached home. Not that Miss Bartleby could have anything to worry about. She patted a golden curl. If Lord Coe was one of those sporting-mad gentlemen who admired athletic pursuits in a woman, however, she would quickly disabuse him of that notion. "La, Miss Ashton is only out seeing about supper." There, let him consider Melody the drudge she was becoming.

Good, maybe someone was taking an interest in the children after all, Corey thought, while his palate reflected on the unlikely combination of well-aged sherry and molasses cookies. "I am relieved."

"You are?" Ah, then he was one of those men who believed women were too weak for lively activities and should merely be decorative. There was none weaker nor more decorative than Felice. She lay back on the loveseat and spread her skirts. "Oh, Miss Ashton is a veritable Amazon."

There was something about the way the chit posed herself that set alarm bells ringing in a wary bachelor's head. Coe had recently seen too many predators at Almack's not to recognize a shark circling for the kill.

"How thoughtless of me, Miss Bartleby," he said,

rising. "With Lady Ashton indisposed and the, ah, maids given time off, I should have realized you were unchaperoned. I wouldn't think of jeopardizing your good name, so I'll—"

"No, you mustn't leave!" The teeth were definitely showing. "Silly me. Of course, I knew you were a gentleman so I had nothing to fear, and now your scruples prove it. A woman cannot be too careful though, can she? I'll just go fetch us someone to play dogsberry"—that brittle laugh again—"while you pour yourself another glass."

Nanny was doing the wash in big tubs out back. Mrs. Tolliver and Meggie were up to their eyebrows in flour. Felice shuddered. "Looks like you're it, Ducky."

Ducky had found his calling. He crooned and rocked, ate cookies and drooled. He played with the silverware and sang *duh-duh-duh* to the viscount's pocket watch. He clapped hands and grinned and enchanted the bemused viscount with sticky hugs. There was no chance for suggestive innuendo, no coy flirtation, no accidental touches—the perfect chaperon. Until, that is, a desperate Felice started sneaking Ducky sips of the wine when she thought the viscount was not looking. When Ducky fell asleep on the sofa, his lordship rose to leave, and no protestations of Felice's could keep him. He was worried about his horse, Corey explained, and feared he had taken too much of Miss Bartleby's time as it was. Further, Miss Ashton was sure to be returning soon. Perhaps he would meet up with her on the path.

Felice held her hand out to be kissed. The viscount shook it, firmly.

Corey leaned against a tree, laughing at his escape. What a hurly-burly household it was, and if that chit wasn't destined to be Haymarket ware, his name wasn't Cordell Coe. But it was, he nodded soberly, and he had a job to do. Naturally he felt like a fool doing it, tromping around the sodden woods looking for a woman he'd never met. His pants were muddied, his boots were ruined, his cravat was spotted with grubby fingerprints, and he swore to conclude his mission before luncheon so he would not have to come back to this raree-show another day.

He quickly tired of shouting "Miss Ashton," but he didn't want to startle her unawares at whatever she was doing—hunting mushrooms, the boys must have meant—so he whistled, feeling even more a jackanapes. At least it wasn't raining.

After four days of rain, Melody thought she'd better take Angie hunting before the hound lost whatever meager understanding she possessed about the purpose of the exercise. They had come to terms, more or less. Angie could race around yipping and yapping at anything that caught her fancy, as long as she stayed in view. She could sniff any tree or charge any bush. This took no training whatsoever, being the mutt's natural, ungoverned tendencies. If anything jumped, ran, or flew out of the shrubbery, Melody could shoot it. If the quarry slithered or crawled, Angie could keep it. The unorthodox method required no stealth or subtlety, just Melody's skill.

She had graduated to an old hunting rifle, a cumbersome muzzle-loading affair, which unfortunately had such a recoil that Melody was black and blue from practicing with it. Now she wore her father's dun-colored hunting jacket from the attics, with its extra padding at the shoulder. It didn't matter that the jacket had moth holes, or that it reached her knees and the sleeves had to be cuffed; the important thing was that she was protected

80

from more bruises. She wore an old slouch hat low on her head to keep her hair out of her eyes and unentangled in twigs, and the oldest, sturdiest dress she could find, an old black bombazine mourning gown that used to be Aunt Judith's. Rather than ruin any of her shoes, which were too expensive to replace, Melody wore a pair of scuffed workboots found in the stable. So what if they were too big? Angie didn't care.

The dog loved this game, with all the sights and smells. She woofed for the sheer joy of the thing. Melody kept training the gun just above and ahead of wherever Angie barked, concentrating. The girl knew she was an excellent shot, if she could only lift the heavy weapon, brace herself against the recoil, aim, and shoot in time. She also had to miss the silly dog, naturally. Miss Ashton set her entire mind to the task, blocking out everything but the dog's baying and the trigger.

There, Angie's yapping was frenzied. She must really see or smell something this time, just beyond those trees. Melody had to get nearer. Walking on the damp undergrowth, she raised the rifle, disobeying her own rules about taking a firm stance. Angie kept barking, Melody kept getting closer to those trees. Maybe it was a deer. Heavens, did she want to shoot a deer? Then whatever it was started out from behind the trees. Melody sighted down the barrel and squeezed back on the trigger.

The viscount came into the clearing where a dog was making a racket just in time to see an unholy apparition taking aim, not ten feet away. He did what any intelligent soldier would do: he dove for the ground.

Melody was so startled—it was him, wasn't it?— that she lowered the rifle and took a step back, onto a projecting tree root. Her foot slid, she rocked for balance, the gun went off. The recoil sent Melody flat on her back, the wind knocked out of her.

81

While she lay there, too dumbfounded to move, if she could, the viscount pulled himself up and stormed over to her. Befogged, she noted his hair was longer than before, likely to cover the scar, and he was not nearly as tan. He had mud in his boots and down his shirt collar and everywhere in between, and he was in a rage, too, towering over her. His face had improved immeasurably, except for the blood dripping from a crease along his cheek, and so had his vocabulary.

Corey did not seem to recognize her yet, which was not surprising in her disheveled state, but no matter, Melody thought, ignoring his tirade. He had come. By some wild and wondrous miracle, by some joyous, stupendous gift of fate, he had searched out her direction and come after her!

And she'd shot him.

Chapter Eleven

*H*e never helped her up, that hurt the most. No, it hurt more that he never recognized her, when Melody believed she would know Lord Corey anywhere. He never assisted her to her feet, like a gentleman would have a lady, and he never waited for Melody to recover her wits enough to beg his pardon or offer to clean his clothes or have Nanny look at the wound. Before she could garble out even one word of apology or welcome, Corey was gone. He shouted back one final, inexplicable curse: "I would rather burn in hell first, madam, but I shall return to the Oaks at eleven o'clock tomorrow morning, and by God, Miss Ashton, either you or that gallows-bait mother of yours had deuced well better be there to receive me."

Mama was no help. She went into hysterics at the sight of Melody, ashen-faced and mud-covered. All Lady Ashton could howl was, "We're ruined, we're ruined."

"But, Mama, we were ruined long before I shot him."

Then Lady Jessamyn swooned. Possibly she passed out from the amount of purely medicinal spirits she had been imbibing for her nerves, but it was an honest faint. It took the efforts of Melody, Felice, and Nanny to revive her. Of course, Nanny's advice to prepare a speech for the gibbet did not hurry along the dowager's recovery.

"It was only an accident, Mama. I am sure Lord Coe will understand when he has time to reflect. We'll put on our prettiest gowns and ask cook to prepare a special tea and—"

"You widgeon," Lady Ashton sobbed into her handkerchief. "He's not here for tea! His sister was one of the Dower House sponsors. He's here about the money!"

That was indeed the worst hurt: Corey hadn't come to see Melody at all. He had come to accuse her mother of stealing from orphans. First, Melody felt like crawling under a rock. Then, she wished she *had* shot the bounder—not fatally, of course—for thinking such things of Mama. Finally, Melody decided she would just have to be as calm and dignified as possible on the morrow, composedly explaining the situation and her efforts to rectify it. . . . After a good cry tonight.

Lord Coe arrived in state. The villagers' talk be damned, he decided, and he was well past worrying over what his servants thought, not after arriving back at the inn looking as if he'd been set on by footpads. No loose tongues would wag once they were back in London either, not if his retainers wished to keep their positions. He acknowledged a touch of arrogance in wishing to intimidate these scurrilous females with his consequence, taking extra pains with his apparel, wearing dove-gray pantaloons and a new coat of blue superfine. His cravat was precise without being pretentious, according to his man, Bates, who was still ailing, but the diamond stickpin left no doubt as to his worth. Viscount Coe sat very much on his dignity, which ached after yesterday's debacle. That was the other reason his lordship chose the padded squabs of his carriage over Caesar's saddle. The plaster on his cheek also reminded him of the score to settle.

The stairs were washed and swept and there was Harry, scrubbed to an inch of his life, waiting to open the carriage door, then direct the coachman to the stables. Harry's eyes widened appreciatively at the well-matched bays, but he only touched his forelock to the viscount and stood aside.

Lord Coe's knock was answered immediately by a well-padded woman in spotless apron who curtsied, introduced herself as Mrs. Tolliver, the cook-housekeeper, and announced that Miss Ashton was expecting his lordship in the library, if he would please to follow her.

The hall was sparsely furnished, but someone had gathered armloads of wild lilacs, so the house bore their delicate aroma instead of the stale air of an unoccupied dwelling. Mrs. Tolliver stopped at an open door, announced "Viscount Coe, ma'am," and stood aside for him to enter.

He took two steps in and halted. No, it couldn't be. The exquisite woman rising to greet him, with her hair demurely coiled at the nape of her neck and a soft rose crepe gown . . .

"Angel!" he shouted.

Now the dog, locked safely away in the stable all morning, decamped when Harry opened the door. She raced across the unmowed lawn, through the overgrown herb garden, and in by the kitchen door, looking for her mistress. Then 'Angel!' someone called, and for one of the few times in her life, the hound answered to her name. With enthusiasm. Which left dirt, dog hair, and grass stains up and down the viscount's dove-gray pantaloons, along with a generous sprinkling of what is usually found on a stable floor.

So much for dignity, or Melody's intentions to soothe the viscount to a conciliatory frame of mind. He was in a royal temper, and not over a mere dog.

"You? You're Miss Ashton? Congratulations for making a perfect gull out of me! How could I have believed there was such innocence? You are no more than a lying, cheating bitch!"

"And how could I ever have thought you were a gentleman?" she yelled back. So much for quiet explanations.

"What do you know of gentlemen, you jade? I'll have you know I thought you were too pure to offer a slip on the shoulder!"

"You what?" Melody's screech brought Mrs. Tolliver running with a meat cleaver. She looked from her mistress, eyes flashing sparks from behind the desk, toward the viscount, who was still standing, his hands in fists at his side. The cook raised the knife and narrowed her eyes until Coe took the seat opposite Melody's, the old desk safely between them. When the viscount was settled and nonchalantly picking dog hairs off his jacket, Mrs. Tolliver lowered the weapon.

"I'll be back in a minute with the tea things," she told him. It was a warning, not a promise.

"You what?" Melody hissed as soon as Mrs. Tolliver was gone, leaving the door partly open.

"You heard me. I thought you were a lady. One doesn't make improper offers to females of breeding."

"Of all the disgusting, despicable—Why, I wouldn't accept such an offer if you were the last man on earth!"

"And I wouldn't make it if I were! You'd likely murder me in my bed while we were—"

Mrs. Tolliver brought the tea tray then and stayed to fuss with the dish of buttered scones. "One lump or two, my lord?" Melody asked sweetly.

Her face was flushed, and her hair was coming undone, and her chest was still heaving, and the viscount couldn't help thinking how she would look

86

in his bed after all. He sipped his tea and choked. The minx had put at least four cubes in his cup. Corey smiled for Mrs. Tolliver's benefit; he'd drink the sugary brew if it killed him. Yes, life would be interesting with Angel in his care. She might poison him, but he would never be bored.

"Another biscuit, milord?" Mrs. Tolliver offered.

"Yes, thank you. Delicious," he replied, but he was watching Miss Ashton lick crumbs off her lip, and his smile widened. His Angel, whom he had never managed to put out of his mind, was one and the same as the corrupt, conniving Miss Ashton. A fallen angel, indeed! As soon as this other matter was concluded . . . He replaced his cup on the tray.

Mrs. Tolliver left with a minatory glance at the nob who seemed to be devouring her mistress with his eyes. "I'll be just outside the door, miss."

Melody should not have had the scone, for it was stuck in her throat, or maybe that was a sob. She would not, not ever, cry in front of this imperious, sanctimonious lecher. She reclaimed her self-control, straightened her posture, firmed her chin.

"Now, my lord," she declared coolly, "now that we have positively ascertained that you have not come to Copley-Whitmore to offer me carte blanche, perhaps you will explain exactly why you are here."

"Cut line, ma'am. You know damn well I came for the child."

Whatever Melody might have expected, and truly she was beyond anticipating any of this improbable conversation, that was not it.

"You came to adopt a child?" she asked in disbelief. What would a degenerate seducer want with a child, and how could he think anyone would consider him a fit parent? "Why, pigs would fly before I let you near one of the little ones."

He colored at that, but replied, "Give over, do, Miss Ashton. We both know I don't mean *a* child, I mean *the* child you have in your greedy clutches."

"Greedy? Why, I'll have you know how hard I have been trying. I gave up my—"

One long-fingered hand waved dismissively. "Spare me the histrionics, Miss Ashton. I've seen how you live. I have also met your mother here and there over the years. I do not know what rig you have been running, but you will not get another groat from me or my sister. Nor will there be the least hint of scandal touching my family name."

"Oh, it's fine to drag my name through the dirt as bachelor fare, so long as no mud rubs off on you and yours. Is that it, my lord?"

"No, Miss Ashton, that's not it at all. Your family *has* no name to speak of, unless you consider blackmailer and extortionist enviable designations."

"Blackmail?"

"Please, Miss Ashton, that wide-eyed innocence won't wash; I won't fall for the same faradiddles twice. Now, I am growing weary of these little games, so shall we place our cards on the table? You have in your dubious care a child, a girl, I believe, whose provision my sister has been supporting with, I might add, ample remuneration for your debatable efforts. The point is moot. Such monies were not enough to satisfy you, and you sought to embarrass my family by publishing the child's existence, unless, of course, your silence was rewarded. Have I stated the problem succinctly enough? Here is an equally simple solution: you will hand over the child without any more roundaboutation, or I shall immediately bring charges against you and your mother for extortion, with your own letters as evidence. I believe blackmail is a deportable offense."

Blackmail? Melody sank back in her seat, trying to make sense of his words. That part about extortion had to be an error, a misunderstanding. There was obviously a child, however, whose very being must not be disclosed, or Lord Coe would not be

88

here. The child was plainly a by-blow then, and—
Poor Meggie. It had to be the wispy little girl with
hair so light she'd reminded Melody of Corey instantly. Meggie's eyes were more turquoisy, she reflected, and the child's makeup held nothing of the
rugged vitality of this man who sat at ease across
from Melody, idly brushing at his waistcoat, waiting for her reply. How very sad it was for little
Meggie to be the unfortunate bastard of such an
uncaring, heartless libertine. She would have done
better as an orphan.

"Well, Miss Ashton, if you have completed your
survey, may I have my answer?"

"No. That is, the answer is no, my lord. I shall
not put a small child into your care. Why, I don't
think you even know her name."

His lordship looked away from those intent green
eyes. "No, that was not in my information."

"It is Margaret. We call her Meggie."

"My mother's name was Margo. Blast it, stop
looking at me like that. I did not even know of the
chit's existence till two weeks ago!"

Worse and worse. "Let me understand. You
abandoned your own flesh and blood like an old hat,
letting your sister assume responsibility, and now
you think you can just come fetch her as if she were
a package lost in transit? And you call me names?"

"Confound it, girl, I am not going to sell my . . .
my ward to white slavers, you know! I planned to
send—to take her to my sister's old governess in
Cornwall."

"Where she will be mewed up with an old woman
instead of here, where she has playmates and people who love her. I think not, Lord Coe. Further,
you cannot have considered the journey." She knew
he hadn't, likely intending to ship a frightened,
homesick waif off with servants. "Meggie has a
weak chest. Would you know what to do if she

started wheezing at night or her lungs became congested?"

She knew dashed well he didn't, the little witch, Corey fumed. Oh, there were hired nursemaids and private physicians, and taking the trip in easy stages, which could take weeks. Weeks in a closed carriage with an ailing, tearful child who would most likely be motion sick the entire journey. Gads, what a coil. Still, he was not leaving any of his kin with these vultures. "I can handle it, Miss Ashton," he blustered. "Just what do you think I am?"

So she told him. She started with reckless reprobate and went on to debauched womanizer, with stops at self-righteous sapskull and buffle-headed bounder. She was paying him back for all of his hateful accusations and disrespect and a few shattered dreams.

The viscount responded in kind, to the mayhem this woman had brought into his life, as well as a few disillusions of his own. They were both on their feet shouting. Miss Ashton was pounding the shaky, old desk and ranting about kettle-calling, and his lordship was wringing an imaginary neck between his hands, raving about bedlamites and blood money.

Mrs. Tolliver slammed a tray of wine bottles and glasses on the desk between them and stood there glowering. "The twins have more decorum than you two," she muttered. "Lucky for you Nanny's not here. You're not too old to have your mouth washed out with soap, either of you. Such talk, Miss Melody!" She crossed her hands over her chest and positioned herself near the door, obviously on guard duty.

His lordship was restored to better humor by the humbling effect of old retainers, that and Miss Ashton's mortification at being caught out as a fishwife. She was blushing furiously, starting just above the rose crepe gown's neckline.

"So your name is Melody," he said pleasantly,

when he could tear his eyes away. "I wondered. Angel doesn't seem quite appropriate, under the circumstances."

"My name is Miss Ashton," she snapped back.

Corey raised one eyebrow in mild rebuke. He was doing *his* part to make polite conversation for her employee's benefit. He lifted his glass. "Melody suits you."

"Not at all, my lord." He wanted polite conversation; he would get polite conversation. "It was a conceit of my father's, who fancied he heard a nightingale sing on the day of my birth. I must be content he did not name me for the bird." She sipped her wine. "I myself have no talent in that direction. I was never permitted to sing in choir and was always delegated page turner at instrumental recitals. So you see, my lord," she said triumphantly, "you do not know me at all. Your impressions are quite, quite wrong. As are your accusations. You have tried and convicted me without a hearing. If it were up to you, I would hang."

"No, ma'am, hanging's too good for you." Then he raised his hand. "But hold, let us not go round Robin's barn again. I hoped to resolve this matter with the least bother to everyone, but I see it will have to be decided by cooler heads. There is a simple question of who has legal right to the child. I'll have my man-at-law look into it, and recommend you do the same." Now victory was his, Corey was sure. The weight of justice almost always came down on the side of money, power, and prestige. "I am confident they will find that no magistrate in his right mind would name a skitter-witted shrew and a schoolroom miss as legal guardians to helpless babes."

"And I am equally as certain no one would entrust the care of a guileless child to a—"

Mrs. Tolliver cleared her throat and jerked her head toward the door. The conversation was over.

91

Chapter Twelve

*M*ama was wrought. Not distraught or over-wrought, just wrought. "Do you mean all this time no one thought I was misusing the donations? And here I've fretted myself to flinders over nothing."

"Mama, blackmail isn't nothing." They were in Lady Ashton's bedroom, and for a change Melody was limp on the chaise after the morning's encounter with Lord Coe, while her mother paced in agitation.

"But I didn't do it, you goose. And how anyone could have thought I would is beyond me. Why, I've had more family skeletons locked away here than many a crypt, with nary a sound of rustling bones heard in the ton. I suppose that's why Lady Pa—ah, Lady Smith cut me dead at the Arbuckles' affair. After that a lot of my friends would not recognize me. I'll just have to write to Lady, ah, Smith and tell her that her little secret, or secrets, are safe with me."

"So the twins are bastards, too?" Melody asked weakly.

"Love children, dear, not that nasty term. And

the twins were to be the tokens of affection presented to a very famous general by his fond, but childless, wife. Unfortunately, the twins' conception did not quite correspond to the general's leave time, and the lady feared he would not appreciate the effort made on his behalf. One child perhaps, but two . . ."

Melody fanned herself with an issue of *La Belle Assemblée* nearby. Much more of this and she would be helping herself to the cordials. "Mama, are none of the orphans, ah, orphans?"

Lady Ashton stopped at her mirror to think, checking for new wrinkles. "We did have a boy once whose parents both died in an influenza epidemic. His grandfather didn't want a child around. I suppose he was the only true orphan."

"Then all of the others are love children?"

"Why, no. Ducky isn't, for one. He's a duke. Why do you think Nanny calls him Ducky?"

"Mama, have you been at the decanters so early this morning?"

"Well, he would have been. He could never have taken on the duties, however. Could you see Ducky in ermine at court? His parents had him declared incompetent and disinherited in favor of the younger son. All legal and all very quiet, and happy they were to get rid of him.

"Pip has quite legitimate parents, also, although I cannot consider them natural parents. We are used to dear Pip by now, of course, but he really is disfigured, you know. His mother took one look at the infant and went into strong hysterics. She said it was a mark of the Devil and refused to keep him. How one can refuse one's own flesh and blood is beyond belief. But she made her husband's life so miserable, down on her knees night and day, that he finally brought the baby to Judith."

There was a catch in Melody's voice as she asked, "Does Pip know?"

"Yes, his father told him. The man used to come visit. He'd cry and carry on about wanting his son at home, and then cross himself. Judith told him to send the checks instead."

"Good for Aunt Judith! But Mama, Aunt Judith was always such a high-stickler, how could she have, you know, taken in the by-blows?"

"Look at that, another gray hair. All this worrying is sending me to an early grave, Melody. What was that? Oh, the children. Well, Judith already had Felice, as a favor to the nabob. The mother left her on Barty's doorstep before joining a traveling company. He couldn't take a babe to India, naturally, and his family had just disowned him. As for the other children, it wasn't *their* fault, you know, that they should suffer for their mamas', um, minor indiscretions. Judith saw it as an act of philanthropy, as long as the children were handsomely provided for, of course. I mean, we could not afford to be that generous. The Dower House children were lucky in that their mothers chose to see them well cared for, if out of sight."

"Oh, so you and Aunt Judith were providing a public service?"

"Sarcasm is not becoming, Melody. We did nothing to be ashamed of, and we did find as many real homes for them as we could. Do you think the children would have done better in foundling homes? Infants there rarely make their first birthday; if they do, they are turned into thieves and pickpockets. What of a child like Harry, who was the chance product of a thunderstorm and a handsome Irish groom? Would you see him sold to a sweep or apprenticed in a mine? Should Meggie have been given to gypsies just because she was born on the wrong side of the blanket? And even Ducky, with his parents married at St. George's, in front of the entire beau monde, he would have ended up in Bedlam, or kept behind locked doors, if not for us."

94

"But couldn't their mothers keep them? Some of them?"

"Don't be naive, Melody. We are talking about well-born ladies, not peasant girls whose fathers find them a husband with the aid of a pitchfork. Ladies don't have a lot of options. Peers want their titles passed through their own bloodlines, not an Irish groom's. And if an unmarried woman is considered even slightly fast, she will never get a respectable offer."

Melody understood that fact all too well, not that she would ever tell Mama about her very dishonorable offer. She would have spasms for sure. "It's all so sad."

"Should the children never have been born, then? Or should moonlings like Ducky be put out for the wolves like the Romans did? Or was that the Greeks? I've never been sure, and I do not think there are any wolves in England anyway. No, high-bred ladies are permitted their genteel riding accidents, of course, but accidents cannot be counted on to cure all of these, ah, indispositions. The muslin company is luckier. They seem to have apothecaries and physicians who . . ." Lady Ashton finally realized she was talking to her own chaste young daughter who should know nothing of such matters. Of course, if other chaste young maidens knew a little more . . . "No matter. We were able to see to the ladies' needs: give them a nice quiet spot where they could say they were visiting a sick relative, and then assure them that their infants and their guilty secrets were both safe. Until now."

Lady Ashton had found a wrinkle that needed attention; she sat at her dressing table trying to decide which lotion to apply. It was Melody's turn to pace.

"So who do you think is sending demand letters to the parents? For that matter, who else had the information?" Melody was positive she could not clear their name without finding the one responsible. She didn't care if there was never another donation, and heaven knew they did not need any more "orphans." But, and it was a very important but, she just had to prove a certain judgmental viscount wrong.

According to Lady Ashton, Mr. Hadley held most of the legal documents, but he had been offering to lend money this age, rather than trying to collect his modest fees. Mama even suspected him of once having a secret *tendre* for her sister Judith. One could just as likely suspect Nanny or Mrs. Tolliver, which is to say, not at all. Both formidable women had been with the family forever, and both had pensions from Judith Morley put away for their old age, which was now. They chose to stay on out of love or duty, assuredly not for the profits. As for the orphans, and Melody refused to think of them any other way, they had the most to lose by such a scheme. Perhaps a maid had come upon Lady Ashton's records while cleaning, Melody suggested, and thought to better her position in the world by bargaining with the information. But Lady Ashton rejected the idea: the maids were all local girls who could not read. Besides, there were no records as such; Lady Ashton kept most of it in her head, to Melody's dismay. If Mama kept emptying wine bottles at such a rate, either the whole county and half of the next would be knowing her secrets, or they would be lost forever. Hopefully fuller documentation was kept with Mr. Hadley—and maybe some less scrupulous person in that office had access to them. Melody would have to check.

"Someone like Edwin? Hadley's been hiring Dower House boys since the start.

"Don't take on so, Melody. I'll simply write to all of the sponsors. We'll be merry as grigs in no time, and we can start planning your come out."

Somehow Melody did not think it would be quite that easy, not if any of the other patrons were anything like Viscount Coe. Which reminded her that she still had to deal with that implacable, infuriating gentleman.

"Mama," she asked, "who *is* legal guardian to the children? I'll go speak to Mr. Hadley tomorrow—you said he had papers and things drawn up—but can the viscount take Meggie?"

"Guardian? Let me see . . . Judith used to have the children named her wards, so I suppose I inherited them along with the Oaks and the dower house. Later I recall Hadley suggesting a man be appointed as trustee, so I believe we entered Bartleby's name. I can't be sure. You know I am not good on details. Quite frankly, the issue has never come up. No one ever wanted one of the brats back."

Mama was fatigued after writing two letters. "Be a dear, Melody, and run these into the village. I want them to go out with the afternoon post. I shall complete more after my nap."

Melody wanted nothing more than to take a page from Lady Ashton's book and lie down with a damp cloth over her eyes. If she couldn't see the confusion around her, maybe it would go away. No such luck. Lady Ashton was suddenly concerned that the letters might go astray, that some miscreant would read the addresses. Previously she had entrusted the mail to the children, or Cook, or any passing carter making deliveries. No more.

So Melody trudged into town. The dog, Angie, followed behind her, still in disgrace. "No, you cannot come. Go home. Bad dog."

So the dog slunk along, further back, until she spotted a way to regain her favored post. What would appease Mistress more than supper, laid right at her feet? Unfortunately Angie's choice of easy pickings had other ideas. The prey, Mrs. Donzell's fat, furry, and much loved Persian cat, was sitting in the sun on the basket of folded laundry, while Mrs. Donzell hung a fresh batch.

So Angie had a row of claw marks across her snout, Mrs. Donzell had to do the entire day's washing over, and Melody had to promise one of the young porkers in recompense.

Harry secreted the squealing piglet away in a sack while the twins were at lessons, but Pip had been too diligent in teaching them their numbers. Laura and Dora were all set to raise a search party to scour the woods for their missing charge; Melody considered letting them go, then decided she couldn't be so craven. With great diplomacy and more trepidation, she explained about the cat, the wash, the damage. The dog and cat fight couldn't come close in volume or intensity to the twin tantrums Miss Ashton was subjected to. She only wished Mrs. Donzell were here to toss dirty wash water over these two creatures. Finally she had the girls quiet enough to listen to her speech that the pigs were, after all, not pets but a commodity. Everyone at Dower House depended on them, Melody said, and Laura and Dora nodded calmly.

Until Mrs. Tolliver announced ham sandwiches for lunch.

Like Chinese torture, the day kept dripping down more woes.

"I have settled with Mrs. Donzell, Mr. Pike," Melody told the constable when he caught up with her while she was checking on the hens, "so there was no reason for you to make the call."

The scurvy little man's watery eyes lit up. "More trouble with the dog, eh? I'll be having you up on charges of harboring a dangerous animal, I will."

Melody sighed wearily. "In faith, Mr. Pike, have you nothing better to do than harass honest citizens?"

"Honest, is it?" he needled, wiping his nose on

98

the back of his sleeve. "Honest folks don't go around shooting peers of the realm."

"Did that dastard bring charges then? I'll counter with trespassing, and—"

"Not yet he didn't, although there be a lot of talk Hazelton way." Pike laid his hand on her arm. "I just thought I'd renew my offer, put in a good word with the magistrate for you, don't you know."

Melody looked down at his hand, with its dirty, chewed fingernails and grime-encrusted knuckles. She spoke slowly: "Mr. Pike, if you and your filth are not out of here instantly, I shall go to the magistrate myself. I am sure Uncle Charles will be interested to learn how the county's business is conducted."

"Uncle Charles, is it?" he groused, but the hand was removed before another foul breath passed his lips. "You think to impress me, miss? Well, you won't get around old Frederick Pike so easy. I know what's what, and I knows you ain't above the law. Your fancy airs ain't worth pig swill. What'd you think, your ma found you under a cabbage patch? You're just another of the freaks and bastards she keeps around the place, and no better'n you should be."

If Melody had just slapped the makebate, she would have brushed through. Heaven knew the loose screw had been slapped many a time. What made it worse, and made Frederick Pike her enemy for life, was that she smacked him in full sight of Harry and Pip and Meggie. They could not hear the awful words, but they certainly had a good view of her hand flying forward, his head snapping back, and his rat-colored wig flying into the chicken coop.

Chapter Thirteen

$\mathcal{L}$ong journeys could be conducive to deep thinking, especially if the carriage was well sprung and comfortable, the scenery was monotonous, and one's traveling companion had all the conversation of a plaster saint. Viscount Coe's man, Bates, wore the same long-suffering expression of many a martyr, but not a word of complaint would pass his lips. He would not mention two complete sets of fine clothing, ruined, nor the boots he'd labored so lovingly over, destroyed, nor all of the extra work involved for a loyal retainer just up from his sickbed. Bates would certainly not comment on his employer's distressing habit of having his face rearranged, nor the viscount's failure to discuss the circumstances of the past days with his devoted, faithful aide. There being nothing else on Bates's mind, however, he sat like a carving.

The viscount had a great deal on his mind, and except for an occasional sigh or sniffle from the wounded valet, he was free to let his thoughts wander. The coach headed toward London; Corey's thoughts wended back to Copley-Whitmore.

Melody. It did suit her. She was like a song that kept repeating in his head. He might not like the tune, nor admire its lyrics or tempo, but he could not forget it. The vision of an angel tenderly wiping his forehead fought with the picture of the fierce Miss Ashton nearly blowing his head off. She was magnificent in a rage, all fire and cutting ice, and she was adorable pretending to be a lady presiding at tea. A contrary animal, was his Miss Melody Ashton. Corey smiled, for there was no doubt about it, Miss Ashton was destined to be his. He could finally admit to the thoughts he'd held all along, from the first moment he had seen her at Barstow's inn: the viscount wanted that young beauty the way he'd wanted his first pony, with every fiber of his being. And now she could be his.

Lord Coe was not sure how he was to accomplish it, with so many guardians protecting the treasure. A man did not usually have to worry about seducing a woman with her mother nearby, much less a cook and a nanny, but he would do it. After all, Melody was not in any position to refuse. She had no name, no money, no future but hardship, and without his protection could be sent to gaol at any time.

Corey was not quite as certain of Melody's guilt as he had been. Oh, she had to be involved in the skullduggery to some extent, but she either had to be a consummate actress or the world's most inept blackmailer, and Lord Coe had difficulty believing either. Miss Ashton had to have known he would come down hard for possession of the child, but she never even opened negotiations. And there was that crack-brained notion of hers that the chit was his by-blow. A lot of men left their butter stamp around the countryside—not that he was one of them— without society's reproach and without their sisters

101

paying leech fees on them, to Corey's sure knowledge. Only a moralist or an innocent would have thought otherwise. Corey smiled again. Or a woman who had already been approached by a—what had she called him?—a vile seducer. He hadn't disabused her of either opinion, his pursuit or his paternity. The first was obvious, and the second was insurance if by some improbable odds Miss Ashton really was unaware of Meggie's parentage.

No child of his would ever be called by such a common-sounding name. Meggie suited an upstairs maid. Margaret was more fitting for a nobleman's daughter, and that's what Lord Coe would call the lass when he went back to fetch her. But what in bloody hell did he know about children anyway, and sickly ones at that? Corey congratulated himself that he hadn't done too shabbily with Ducky—talk about names for aristocratic offspring!—and he had actually enjoyed horse-mad Harry and serious Philip. Maybe children were not such an affliction after all. Even the impish little twins were appealing, making him regret not having a glimpse of his new ward. Erica would have wanted to know, he convinced himself. Of course, he would never tell his sister the chit was frail. He'd say she was delicate and sweet and pretty, but lively, just the way he imagined a daughter should be, now that he was imagining. If a man were to have a daughter, of course. Getting Margaret to Cornwall was still no attractive prospect, but a son of his own mightn't be such a bad idea, someday.

The trip to Cornwall might not look inviting, but the return to Copley-Whitmore did. As usual these days, Corey's mind quickly reverted to thoughts of Melody. As soon as he had papers in hand to guarantee Margaret's future under his protection, he'd see about offering a different type of protection to Miss Ashton.

Perhaps he should bring a gift when he returned,

102

something unexceptional for the mother's sake, to show that it was possible he had been overhasty in his judgments. It was premature for the emeralds those green, green eyes demanded. Lord Coe smiled on his side of the carriage, picturing Melody decked in emeralds and little else.

There, look at him grin, Bates grumbled to himself, sitting stoically rigid on the other seat. He's likely figuring a way to destroy more of his fine clothes.

Lord Coe's solicitor was not encouraging about speeding up the wheels of justice.

"No, a woman cannot adopt a child, or be named as trustee for a minor if property is involved. However, a man need only be named for the courts while the female is de facto guardian. Often the male dies, and no substitute is named. The courts are very overburdened with these matters, you must know. If there are no complaints, there is no inquiry.

"However," he went on, "in the hypothetical case you mentioned, there may or may not be accurate and complete filings whatsoever. Highly irregular situation from the start. I would have to direct a clerk to wade through court documents of the year and month in question. You don't have those details, my lord, for the, ah, hypothetical infant? In that case, I would send a man to the county of residence to search parish records, barring, of course, the cooperation of the *litage's* man-at-law. This could take time."

"If your man finds that the woman in question does have some trumped-up right to the child, how can that be overturned? Assuming for the sake of discussion, of course, that the person seeking custody is a legitimate relative of the child. Legitimate may be the wrong word. Blood kin, then."

"Quite, quite. Nearly every decision of the courts can be reversed, but often at unforeseen expense."

103

"Dash it, I'm not a nipfarthing! That is, the hypothetical gentleman does not consider the price of moral justice."

"Forgive me, Lord Coe, I had not meant mere financial expense, although justice is often hurried along by such means. I was thinking of the personal cost. If the gentleman in question were to present such papers to the higher court, seeking to rescind a legal adoption, there would have to be just cause, charges of neglect or whatever, an examination, proof of his prior claim, et cetera. There would be no way to keep said gentleman's name out of the public eye. The press, you know. I don't think that's what you want."

"B'gad, no!"

"Then I suggest I send a man to ascertain the details, and feel out the possibility of quiet negotiations."

Quiet negotiations, with Miss Ashton? Crocodile-legged sofas would get up and walk away first. Coe wished the man luck.

"I'm sure we can have the matter neatly wrapped up in, say, a month, my lord."

Coe gave him two weeks and left.

Two weeks before he would see ... the child, of course. Two weeks in London at the height of the Season, acquaintances everywhere, entertainments and invitations too numerous to count, and Lord Coe had nothing to do. Idly, he directed the coachman to drive to Kensington, too abstracted to recall that he'd given Yvette her *congé* and was now keeping a pretty little ladybird in rooms off King Street.

"But *mon cher*, you give Yvette permission to stay on here another month, *non*? Ah, you've changed your mind and wish Yvette to remain, *oui*?"

Non. But Corey could not come right out and say he'd forgotten and arrived in Kensington out of habit, not after Yvette's new protector had left in such a hurry, diving out the back door when Coe stepped through the front. Some protector. Now that Corey did remember dismissing Yvette, he also recalled leaving her a handsome enough parting gift that she need not settle for such a paltry fellow. He felt less gauche.

"I, ah, just wanted to talk. Is that all right?" He fully intended to pay for her time.

"Talk? You want to talk to Yvette?" She shrugged. One received strange requests in her line of work. "But of course, *cheri*, now that you have chased away that *chien*, what else is there to do?" She languidly bestowed herself on the divan, allowing the neckline of her robe to fall open. Not that the frothy, pink garment concealed much of Yvette's charms anyway, being nearly transparent.

Coe expected to be interested, and wasn't, to his own surprise. He still wanted to know her opinions, however, on matters about which he definitely could not approach females of his own class. It occurred to him that, man of the world or not, he was woefully ignorant about certain facts of life. "Yvette, what would you do if you found yourself with child?"

She looked at him as if he'd grown another head. *"Enceinte, moi?* With your child?"

"No, no, just a hypothetical child."

"Me, I do not know this hypothetical."

"Um, just the child of any man, no one in particular," Corey explained.

Yvette drew herself up, and her robe closed. "Me, I always know the man. I am not, how do you say, Covent Garden ware, going with any man for the price." Her price just went up.

"My pardon, *cherie*. What if, then, it were my child, or the man who just left? What would you do?"

"Me, I would not be such an *imbecile* in the first

105

place. But if, yes, if such a thing should happen, *incroyable*, I would take care of it."

"But would you discuss it with me, with the father? Would you hold him responsible?"

Yvette laughed. "Ah, finally I see. Some *jeune fille* is looking to net the so-handsome, so-wealthy *vicomte*. That is the oldest trap since the apple, *non*? No, *monsieur*, Yvette would not lay such a snare. That is not what you English call pound dealing, *n'est-ce-pas*? If I found myself in such a temporary embarrassment, I might ask *monsieur* for assistance, since you have been so generous, but no, I think not even then. I would simply get rid of *l'enfant* as soon as possible, if not before. A woman in my position cannot afford to lose her looks or so much of her time. The gentlemen, they forget, you see, if a woman goes visiting away too long. But no, no, and no, I would not spread a noose for one such as you, demanding marriage. Yvette knows the rules."

"Then I would never know?" Somehow the idea did not sit well with him.

"But what's to know? *Un homme* comes to Yvette for pleasure, not morning sickness and the shape of a cow. He has a wife for that. *Alors*, enough of this so-foolish talk you call hypothetical. Yvette is much better at the pleasure, *oui*?"

Oui, but not today.

Two weeks in town. Lord Coe had dinner at his club, checked the betting book to make sure his name wasn't in it, heard the latest *on dits*, and was happy his name wasn't among those either. Later he went to the opera, where his newest mistress—there, he recognized her in the first row of dancers—curtsied to his box during the tenor's solo. The bucks in the pit whistled till he bowed, and the turbanned dowager in the next box clucked her disapproval. "Disgusting," she declared loudly to the younger woman next to her, a washed-out wisp of a thing in a faded gown that advertised a poor relation or a paid companion.

So Corey bowed to the matron and blew a kiss to the companion. After that they left him alone with his thoughts: of men like apes beating their chests, flaunting their possession of women, of women who had no knowledge of love, and women who had too much. He thought of men who craved heirs and begot bastards, and women who threw out children like the trash, women who feared losing their looks, ladies who feared losing their reputations, and a girl who truly seemed to care about the innocent ones. He thought about the children.

Dammit, why should he wait two weeks? He could help the solicitor's man check records, he could help sweet-talk the Ashtons into parting with Margaret. What a brilliant idea, and the one he wanted all along!

Corey almost convinced himself that he should be in Copley-Whitmore for the child's sake; it was his duty to ensure her welfare. Never before had duty and desire combined so happily

He left the opera house after leaving a check with the stageman. His mistress would understand. The green-eyed dasher could dance, but he bet she could not fire a rifle.

Bates was muttering over the packing—doubles of everything if they were going back to that hell-hole—when the anguished letter came. Coe's sister, Erica, was in despair at not hearing from him and had decided to take matters into her own hands, despite his orders to stay away. The peagoose was going to Copley-Whitmore. She was leaving Bath in ten days. Blast, he had enough to worry over without another totty-headed female on his hands. She would only be overemotional about the child, possibly growing attached to the chit, and her very presence in that vicinity could give rise to the same conjecture he was trying to avoid. In addition, having his sister about would certainly cramp Lord Coe's efforts in Miss Ashton's direction. The mother and nanny and cook were bad enough.

Erica was usually the most biddable of females, Corey reflected, until she dug her heels in. Only once before had she disregarded his advice and look where that got her. Perhaps his advice hadn't been so fine, landing her with that mawworm Wooster, but Corey was young then and had done his best to see her settled before he had to join his cavalry unit. Age and good intentions were no excuses, he knew, and by Jupiter he was trying to make that up to her—if she would only stay out of it!

There was no dissuading her, Coe knew, although he wrote an impassioned letter anyway. Damn, she would be singled out in that backwoods neighborhood of dubious repute like a goldfish in a bowl of guppies . . . unless Corey managed to muddy the waters. He interrupted Bates to order out his evening clothes.

There must be hunting or fishing, and assemblies at Hazelton, and picnics . . . He could invite the Cheynes and the Tarnovers for respectability. Lady Tarnover had a stepbrother in politics. There was that prosy bore Pendleton, and Major Peter Frye, Coe's good friend, could be counted on to do the pretty. Frye had a ne'er-do-well cousin who was always on repairing leases. The basket scrambler would be sure to dangle after Felice and her tales of the nabob's money. Corey wondered who else might be at White's, who else would be interested in his sister or a fortnight's house party at a decrepit estate on the way to nowhere.

That climber Lady Ashton would be delighted with the company, Harry would be thrilled with all the horses, and Miss Ashton would be livid, which would be nothing new. No matter, Corey would have nearly a month to bring her round. Just in time for that little house in Kensington to be vacant again!

Chapter Fourteen

"*Y*ou want *how* much for this wreck of a place, Miss Ashton? Perhaps you misunderstood me. I only wish to rent the Oaks for a month, not purchase it."

"I understood your wish, my lord, but not your reason. If you think to turn my family home into a place for your . . . your orgies, I won't have it."

"Miss Ashton, when I choose to hold an orgy, you will be the first to know."

Melody's furious blush reminded the viscount he had vowed not to rush his fences with her. "But the Oaks will take an additional outlay to bring it to the standards of a gentleman's residence."

"Gentleman, hah!" That was eloquent enough of Melody's opinion of the devilish rogue in front of her, his pale hair slightly tousled from the ride, his teeth gleaming in a bright smile, and his slightly crooked nose adding even more character to a face that—No, Miss Ashton told herself. This will never do. "The price is firm."

Lord Coe also recalled he had vowed not to lose

his temper with the prickly wench. "Very well, ma'am, I accept your terms, but it is highway robbery."

"Ah, that was one of the few crimes of which you have yet to accuse me. Let me see, there was lying, cheating, blackmail, wantonness, and attempted murder. Am I next to be called traitor to king and country?"

"I don't know. Have you been selling state secrets to eke out the egg money?"

"My lord, I don't know any state secrets, and I do not know what you are doing here." Melody had received the infuriating man's note asking to call, and she had met him outside, intending to be courteous but brief. Meggie had a legal male guardian, such as he was: old Toby had put his *X* on the paper under Mr. Hadley's signature. This blackguard standing close to her—too close—on the Oaks' front steps, dressed to the nines and obviously determined to tease her out of the sullens, was not entitled to Meggie, nor to any of Miss Ashton's good humor.

"I told you, I was concerned for the child's welfare."

"Gammon. The child is six years old, and you have never given a ha'penny's thought to her before."

"Ah, but you yourself reminded me so charmingly of my responsibilities." His smile broadened. "Furthermore, I did wish to apologize for that other day. Some of my charges may have been unfounded, some of my words hasty."

Some? Unfortunately, Melody had to admit that some were likely all too true. He was certainly being noble about it; she could be no less a lady. "And I, too, owe you an apology. It seems there may indeed be something untoward going on, so your concern was—is—understandable. Please be assured

110

that my mother and I had no knowledge of such a scheme, and we are trying to take steps."

His blue eyes fairly sparkled. "There, I knew we could see eye to eye about something! Now if we are decided that you aren't a blackmailer, and I am not a debaucher"—he thought he heard Melody mutter something about that wasn't what she'd decided at all—"might we call a truce and go inside where we could be more comfortable while we let the solicitors handle the question of the child? I really would like to discuss my plans for the house and enlist your aid in a scheme of my own."

Outside in the fresh air was close enough for Melody's comfort, but she could not continue to be so ragmannered in the face of his polished charm. She led the way to the library, and Angie came gamboling after the viscount.

Mindful of his buff kerseymere breeches, and Bate's sorrowful demeanor on learning his master's destination, the viscount commanded, "Down, sir!" in his best battalion voice.

"It's a female," Melody corrected.

"Figures," Corey replied, but his grin overrode the insult.

They were both amazed when the hound actually stopped frolicking around and flopped herself down at Lord Coe's feet. Impressed despite herself, Melody offered the viscount a glass of wine, and he drank in the sight of her in a muslin gown embroidered with violets, gracefully pouring. Her chestnut hair was neatly, severely bound; how he wished to see it loose and flowing down her back. Melody could feel his gaze bringing a warm flush to her cheeks, so she hurriedly took her seat behind the desk, folding her hands in front of her primly, expectantly. Neither one noticed the dog at Corey's feet, contentedly chewing the gold tassels off the lord's brand-new Hessian boots.

"You were going to tell me about a plan of yours,

111

my lord? One that might conceivably explain your wishing to rent the Oaks."

Corey admired how she looked him directly in the eye. For such a young chit she was remarkably self-assured. Of course, Mrs. Tolliver was likely nearby with a cast-iron frying pan. He smiled lazily. "I don't suppose you would swallow a tale about my appreciation for the scenery around here or my need to rusticate?"

Knowing from Felice that he was the *compleat* London beau and from her mother how many country estates of his own he had? Not likely. Melody tried to raise one eyebrow in mocking imitation of his own expression, and only succeeded in scrunching her face and making him laugh. It was a very nice laugh. Her own spirits lightened at the sound.

"There, I've made you smile," he said, as if he cared. "Very well, my sister wishes to see the child she has been supporting all these years. You'll acknowledge her right?"

"Gladly, and I would be happy to express my appreciation for her generosity and beg her pardon that someone has been trying to intimidate her. I am sure my mother would second that and extend an invitation, too. There is no need for you to lease the house." Or cut up Melody's peace, but she did not express that last thought.

"My sister has been blue-deviled lately, and I thought to invite other friends to keep her company, a regular house party, in fact."

"Here, with the children?" Melody remembered Pike's reaction to the orphans, terming them freaks and bastards; she was still agonizing over his specific insults to her. No one would do that to her charges. "I will not have the children laughed at or made the butt of tasteless jokes."

"And I would not have friends who did. There are members of the ton more eccentric and less amiable than Ducky, and many whose parentage does not

112

bear inquiry. You need not be such a tigress, rushing to the defense of her cubs. No one shall harm them. You have my word on that."

Why Melody should trust him was a mystery, but she did. In this, at least. She was not so sure about others of his motives, which prompted her to ask, "And this scheme of yours?"

"Requires your help, and that of the children, of course." He steepled his fingers beneath his chin and spoke in a low, confiding voice. "You see, I wish to find my sister a new husband and need to know if the prospective brothers-in-law like children. I thought to invite some eligible bachelors here, to gauge their reactions. Someone, I don't know who, said you could learn a lot about a man by watching how he treats children and d—Blast this mangy mutt! Look at my boots! Of all the poorly trained, evil-minded—I've a good mind to—"

"Children and ...?" she asked, laughing, and was pleased to see his anger turn to chagrin and then to the good humor that etched lines on his tanned cheeks and made his eyes sparkle. They both agreed the gentlemen would have ample testing ground. His lordship was willing, naturally, to pay for Angie's services as part of the experiment, once the hound had worked off her debt to his man, Bates.

"I am afraid poor Angie will be trying your sister's likely suitors for years, Lord Coe. But if I may ask, has Lady Wooster no preference in this matter?"

Interestingly enough, Corey felt like confiding in Miss Ashton, the same woman whom he had castigated as a lying jade not ten days ago. He did go on to tell about his sister, four year his junior, and how at an early age she had fallen in love with a soldier. Erica's soldier was a penniless second son with no prospects, except an imminent recall to service on the Peninsula. Lord Coe had found the two

113

together—Corey did not mention that he'd found them on the road to Scotland—and sent the young man off with a flea in his ear. The soldier was reported dead or missing shortly thereafter. Inconsolable, Erica went into a decline until a desperate Lord Coe sent her to visit her old governess in Cornwall, for he had to rejoin his own unit.

On Corey's next leave, Erica seemed apathetic, but resigned. She agreed to marry the man of her brother's choice, a solid, wealthy member of Parliament, an older gentleman who would cure her of those romantic flights and see to her welfare. Wooster turned out to be an ogre, who furthermore never gave Erica the children she craved. The only favor he did her was in dying of an apoplexy four years later.

"That was over a year ago, and now that she is out of mourning I want to make it up to her. I have invited an earl, a war hero, and a rising politico, all with impeccable lineage, substantial incomes, spotless reputations."

"But what about love?" Melody wanted to know. "Is there no place for that?"

"My dear, she is a woman of twenty-four summers, not that starry-eyed chit. She has had six or seven years since her childish infatuation, and she's shown no preference for anyone."

"But she was married for four of those years."

"What's that to say to the point? Don't be naive, Miss Ashton. Women of her class"—Melody noted he did not say "your class" or "our class"—"often find love outside of marriage."

"And that doesn't bother you? You would countenance her taking a lover, rather than marrying below her?"

"It's the way of the world, my dear."

It was tragic, that's what it was, and not just for this hard-hearted man's unfortunate sister. Melody vowed to befriend Lady Wooster and defend her against her brother's machinations, if the lady could not like any of his choices.

But what of Melody herself? Every word Corey spoke, every arrogant, aristocratic pronouncement of what was suitable for his family, cut like a knife into Melody's soul. Here he was, laughing with Melody, confiding in her, treating her like a friend, like an equal. But they were not equals and neither, it seemed, could forget that. Melody had no fortune or standing in the ton, her family name was stained with scandal, and now there were doubts about her origins. Oh, she'd hurried to Aunt Judith's family Bible as soon as Pike left, and found her birthday properly recorded. Was she truly going to be eighteen next month? She felt like eighty. But there it was, in Aunt Judith's firm hand. She was not just a foundling from the wayside. There was, however, no record of her parents' marriage. Melody knew there had been a runaway match—everyone seemed to know that—but was there never a wedding to legitimize her parents' love? She couldn't come right out and ask, Mama, did you ever marry my father? so she checked the local church registry one day when she brought flowers for the altar. Nothing. That's what she could hope for from Lord Coe and his sweet, teasing smile: nothing.

Melody was wrong, of course. Seeing shadows come to her eyes and detecting a quiver in her voice when she asked if he would like tea, the viscount was disturbed. He tried joking about the dog, enlisting Miss Ashton's sympathy for his sister, eliciting her advice about readying the Oaks. All he got was cast-down looks, monosyllabic replies, and deference to his wishes, no spark, no lilting laughter, no dimple. This quiet, humble, courteous Miss Ashton was not at all to Corey's liking. She even put the correct lump of sugar in his tea when Mrs. Tolliver brought the tray, nodded, and left. Was

Melody sad to think of strangers in her home? Was she shy about meeting the socialites he'd invited?

When Melody asked if he would like more tea, he absently nodded and held his cup out for her to refill. She had to come around the desk and stand close to him, where he could look up into her melancholy eyes. Hell and damnation, he hated that shattered look!

Therefore, while Melody poured, Lord Coe said, "You know, Angel, if you've had second thoughts about leasing the house, my previous offer still stands."

That was what Miss Ashton could expect from Lord Coe: a slip on the shoulder. She kept pouring the hot tea, while Corey was absorbed in watching the changes of expression flicker across her face, the brows gather, the green sparks shoot from her eyes, the lower lip thrust out. He kept watching. Melody kept pouring: over the brim, over the saucer, over his lap.

Bates was going to be *so* pleased. There was nothing to dampen a gentleman's ardor more than damp nether garments, especially on a long ride on horseback to a disapproving valet who was going to demand some explanation. Yet Lord Coe kept laughing out loud. By George, she was magnificent! What a mistress she would be!

Perhaps the wet unmentionables were interfering with Lord Coe's thinking, or he would have noticed the great gaps in his reasoning. Miss Ashton was such a delight with her candid charm, Corey was now convinced she simply could not be any kind of blackmailer. And there could be no huggermugger with the children's welfare either, she worked so hard for them. If money was in such short supply, Melody could have supported herself by going out for a governess instead of staying to feed the chickens. Only his Angel would turn down his generous offer, preferring to raise pigs!

Now, if she was not a criminal and not a liar, simply a gentlewoman fallen on hard times, then she was indeed a lady, a pure young lady not to be taken advantage of by rakes like Cordell Coe. If she was innocent of wrongdoing, she was innocent of immorality, and innocent she must stay. Reason be damned. Lord Coe was not thinking with his head, and lust knows no logic.

Chapter Fifteen

*W*hatever happened to the so-steady Miss Ashton from Miss Meadow's Select Academy, the one who never played pranks on the teachers or giggled in church or went into alt when Loretta Carmody's Adonis-like older brother took some of the girls out to tea? Sensible, mature Melody Ashton with nary a hair out of place nor an ungraceful gesture was long gone.

Melody felt as sensible as those dratted pigs who wouldn't stay in their pen where they were safe, warm, and well fed. She considered herself as mature as the twins, letting one man send her into a pelter with laughing eyes and roguish looks and suggestions—Well, suggestions that would have Miss Meadow frothing at the mouth. As for being neat as a pin, Melody had on an oversized apron, a borrowed mobcap, and had smudges of dust on her nose. She and Mrs. Tolliver were working with some village girls to get the Oaks ready for his lordship's arrival. In two days, the viscount would be bringing a chef, a butler, footmen, grooms, and his own valet, but Melody had decided that Lord Coe's servants would be as superior as he, and she was determined they find nothing to disparage in her family home. The paper was faded, and the carpets had bare spots, but at least everything would be cleaned and aired.

Melody whomped the pillow in the master bedroom again—his bedroom—and told herself she was being a perfect ninny to let anything about the man affect her so. He would come with his elegant guests, they would keep him occupied and amused, and she, Melody Ashton, would go about her own business, as far away from the disconcerting peer as possible. She would have more time to spend with the children and the garden, now that money was not to be such a worry and she didn't have to fret about putting food on the table. Mrs. Tolliver's niece Betsy was coming to take over cooking chores at Dower House, while her aunt stayed on as housekeeper at the Oaks, and Pip had the bookkeeping well in hand. Melody gave the pillow another hard whack. Yes, she would have plenty of time. It wasn't as if she would be socializing with Lord Coe or his fancy company. Earls—*thump*—and war heroes—*thump*—and diplomats. It was a good thing the ticking held on the pillow, and a good thing Melody Ashton would be seeing so little of that smooth-tongued rake.

"Not socialize with the viscount and his party? Melody, have you been working in that wretched garden again without your bonnet? You must be all about in your head if you think we can let an opportunity like this pass! Why, the Tarnovers and the Cheynes are the crème de la crème. And just think, young bachelors!" Mama was *aux anges*, going so far as to open a bottle of champagne to celebrate. Felice was in the village purchasing new ribbons for her gowns.

119

"But Lord Coe is bringing his own particular friends, Mama," Melody managed to interject. "He cannot wish three women thrust into their midst."

Lady Ashton ignored her. "We cannot invite the whole party here, of course, the children, don't you know. Melody dearest, you shall have to see about keeping the pesky brats out of sight. A picnic, though, would be just the thing. Yes, we shall invite Lord Coe to bring his guests to our picnic, for a start. Unless he asks me to be hostess for him, naturally, then we need not entertain at all. Yes, I think I may even offer, since it would seem peculiar to have another lady in charge at the Oaks."

"He is bringing his sister, Mama," Melody remarked. "Surely she will be hostess enough. And she is coming to see Meggie, remember."

"Don't be tiresome, Melody. And do put some of that strawberry lotion on your face. I swear, you'd let your complexion go all brown and freckled if no one took you in hand. Where was I? Oh yes, Meggie. I do hope she won't have the grippe, or anything, when Lady Wooster comes. You will be sure she makes her proper curtsy, won't you? And then say she has to have lessons or a nap or whatever. No one wants a child underfoot more than ten minutes. I do hope dear Lady Wooster is over her pet about those nasty letters. You did explain that we knew nothing about them, didn't you?"

"Yes, Mama, but I am not sure Lord Coe believed me."

"Of course he did, Melody. Why would he not? And Lady Wooster is a sweet woman, actually rather niminy-piminy if you ask me, so I am sure she won't cut up stiff. Exquisite dresser, too. I wonder if we can convince our viscount to throw a ball."

"Our viscount? Mama, Lord Coe is renting the house; he is not taking on the care and entertainment of three impoverished females. We are his

120

landladies, not his friends! Why, we are not even his social equals."

Lady Ashton was pouring the last glass. It would go to waste, else, all those lovely bubbles. "What's that? Not his equals? I'll have you know the Morleys go back to William the Conqueror, and your father's people were very well respected in Kent."

So well respected that they cut him off without a shilling for running away with Jessamyn Morley. And William the Conqueror also had camp followers. Melody's mother was seeing the world through champagne bubbles, bubbles that would be pricked at the first snub, or when the invitations did not arrive. Poor Mama.

"Perhaps we might see them at church, Mama," she offered. "Or now that we are above oars, perhaps we can contrive to attend the assembly at Hazelton." It was like talking to Ducky.

"Let me see, you'll need a ball gown, and we can all use new frocks for daytime. That new tissue seems perfect for the warmer months, and—"

"No, Mama. You put me in charge, remember? The viscount's deposit money has already been credited to the children's accounts." Melody might not be able to save her mother from making a cake of herself, nor from suffering cuts and setdowns, but she would not permit her mama to play fast and loose with their finances again. The money was in Melody's name, with Mr. Hadley as overseer, and most was earmarked for the children's educations or to restore their bank balances. No one would be able to accuse the Ashtons of living off orphans' shares.

"Not even Ducky's?" Lady Ashton wailed. "What could he need money for?"

"For his future, Mama, especially Ducky. He's never going to be able to earn a living or care for himself. Could you wear a new dress and gaily dance knowing that someday Ducky might be homeless or hungry?"

Easily, but Lady Ashton didn't say so. What she said was: "You know, Melody, I was saving this champagne for your wedding. I'm glad I drank it now, so it won't go to waste."

Later that evening, after dinner and before bedtime, Lady Ashton was in the weepy stage of inebriation. Melody refused to make any push to attach a gentleman, her mother sobbed. She wouldn't dress in the height of fashion, she even intended to refuse invitations. Melody would never get married, the family would never be rich, Lady Ashton would never get to London again. There was no reason to save the champagne.

"How could you be such an undutiful daughter, Melody?" Lady Jessamyn whimpered into her lace handkerchief. "Now I'll never get to see you wearing the family veil I kept safe all these years."

Grateful for any distraction from the tearful diatribe that had been going on since luncheon, Melody asked, "What veil is that, Mama? I never heard of any family heirlooms."

Of course she hadn't. The jewels and portraits had been pawned years ago. One yellowed and frayed piece of lace wouldn't fetch a brass farthing at the cent-per-centers; now it was priceless.

Sniff. "Why, the veil my mother wore at her wedding, and hers before that. To think it will molder in the—"

"Did you wear it, Mama? Did you?"

Lady Ashton looked at her eager daughter in bewilderment. "Of course. Didn't I just say it was an heirloom?"

"But at your wedding, Mama?"

"Why are you such a slowtop tonight, Melody, when I have such a headache? Where else would I wear a wedding veil? And a beautiful bride I was,

122

too. The whole county said so. And to think you'll never—"

A wedding! "Do you know, Mama, I don't believe you ever told me where you and Papa were married."

"Oh, St. Sebastian's in Hazelton. Judith insisted the local chapel would never do. Are you ... could you be interested in weddings? Oh Melody, dearest, please say you'll reconsider!"

Love. Marriage. A baby. What joy! Melody would certainly reconsider her position on meeting the houseguests—and the host. Mama drifted from euphoria to snores, while Melody wondered if there was a way to squeeze a new dress out of the account books she and Pip were so conscientiously balancing. Soon it would be time to sell the pigs, but no, Melody could not purchase a new gown when she'd denied Felice the treat that very evening.

Felice had been furious, accusing Melody of trying to snabble the gentlemen herself.

"All of them?" Melody asked, trying to tease Felice out of the sullens. "I should think with four or five bachelors, even I could not be so selfish."

"You'll never bring him up to scratch, you know," Felice bit back, and they both knew which *him* she meant. Melody blushed furiously and tried to deny any interest in that quarter, but Felice wasn't swallowing that gammon. "Women have been trying for years, fashionable, witty, well-connected women. And all with bigger dowries and better figures." She puffed out her own considerable charms, while Melody's confidence—and chest—caved in. "They call him the elusive viscount," Felice continued, "and his ladybirds are always the highest flyers. Why, his latest—"

Nanny was sitting in the corner with her knitting, and now she cleared her throat with an admonition to Felice to mind her tongue lest it turn black and grow warts and curdle milk. "For it's ugly is as ugly does." She went back to her knitting, a striped affair made of Mrs. Barstow's sister's remnants. Whatever the item was, it would soon rival Joseph's coat.

Felice went back to her grievances. "And I don't see why I cannot have a new gown, even if you aren't interested in making the most of the best thing that's ever happened in Copley-Whitmore. If you want to go around looking like a schoolgirl on holiday or a hired drudge, why should I hide my light under your barrel?"

Melody wished she had a barrel big enough so she could stuff the tiresome girl into it and mail her off to Sir Bartleby, wherever he was. She tried once more to explain that the money wasn't hers, it was to provide for the children. She should have saved her breath.

"I absolutely must have a new dress, Melody."

"Then you shall have to find the money to pay for it. Perhaps Mrs. Finsterer would let you help in the store in exchange for the material."

Melody might have suggested Felice appear in her shift for Lord Coe's guests, so shocked was the other girl. Her baby-blue eyes widened, and her rosebud mouth hung open for a moment, until she recovered. "What a tease you are, Melody," she tittered. When Felice realized Melody was not teasing, and not budging, she demanded a loan of the money. "My father is good for it," she insisted.

It was Nanny who answered: "Your pa's good for nothing but filling your head with moonshine," at which Miss Bartleby flounced off in a huff, leaving Melody to deal with the tea things and Lady Ashton in her cups.

"That one's got the pretty plumes of a peacock and the sharp claws of a hawk," Nanny warned. "You watch yourself there, missy."

"She's just spoiled, Nanny."

124

"Too many cooks, that's what it were. Lady Judith taking her in like the daughter she never had, doting like a hen with one chick, and that nabob with his promises, and then your mama . . . Why, that one's got less sense than the good Lord gave a duck."

"And me, Nanny? What about me?"

"You're in over your head for sure, missy. You're like to drown, too, less you learn to swim mighty quick like. There's big fish in that pond, child, what gobbles little minnows like you. Start paddling."

Chapter Sixteen

She was treading water, that's how Melody felt, holding her breath and getting nowhere. Here she was on the steps of the Oaks, lined up with the others, like so many serfs waiting to pay obeisance to a feudal lord. The village girls were hoping for permanent positions, and Mrs. Tolliver had the chatelaine of office in hand and the light of battle in her eye, waiting for the uppity London servants. Harry and Pip were combed and starched, Harry restless and Pip tense and ready to flee, while the younger children were back at Dower House with Mrs. Tolliver's niece, Betsy. Felice was impatiently twirling her parasol and tugging the neckline of her gown downward. Nanny kept tugging it up, and Melody feared the thin fabric would give out in despair. Lady Ashton, suffering the grandfather of all hangovers, could barely stand. The sun was torturing her eyeballs, and if the pounding in her ears wasn't hoofbeats signaling the viscount's arrival, Lady Ashton warned, she was going to be sick. On second thought, maybe she would be sick anyway.

All Melody could think of was the valet's reaction to that! She bit her lip and fussed with the ribbon threaded through her curls. What in the world would Corey think?

He thought she was enchanting, in her pale blue merino with a sprig of violets pinned to the neckline and her smile, hesitant but welcoming. The sunshine brought out all the red and gold highlights of her hair and added a natural glow to her creamy skin. The viscount also thought her graceful shoulders too slim to bear responsibility for the entire rackety group, so he proceeded to charm each and every one of the greeting committee, to relieve Melody of some of her self-assumed burdens.

He dismissed the hopeful maidservants with a smile and a simple, "If you satisfy Mrs. Tolliver, I am satisfied." For another of those smiles, Melody thought, the village girls would scrub the gates of hell if he asked. Mrs. Tolliver he introduced to his own major domo, who bowed ever so stiffly as he declared himself at her service. Mrs. Tolliver led the London staff away, happily murmuring, "At my service, why, I never!"

Melody thought she saw the viscount wink in her direction and decided the rogue was showing off for her benefit. Still, she breathed more easily.

Lord Coe turned to the boys and asked Harry if he would be kind enough to show the grooms around the stables and possibly help with Caesar. "The stallion gets restless in strange surroundings, and you seem to have a fine hand with him." No words could have thrilled Harry more; Nanny had to call him back to bow to his lordship.

"And Philip, my friend," the viscount said, shaking hands with the solemn lad, "I have a favor to beg of you, also. I brought some books with me that Lady Ashton will not wish mixed up with her own. Dry stuff, history and science, mostly. I understand you are familiar with the Oaks' library, so could I bother you to take charge of the collection, find a spot where they will be out of the way, or even make a list if you think it necessary? In truth, I cannot trust such a task to the footmen."

Pip did his best to stammer out that he would find the project an honor, not a chore. He gave up trying to express himself with manful dignity, when Lord Coe added: "Of course, if any of the volumes should be of any interest to you, feel free to make full use of them." Pip grinned like the young boy he was and flew after a footman toting a heavy carton from the baggage carriage.

Melody knew she was seeing a master in action when Corey bowed again over her mother's hand. "Lady Ashton, how kind of you to meet me in person," he said, still holding that hand, to Lady Jessamyn's giddy delight. "And looking lovelier than ever. Why, if I hadn't known Miss Melody was your daughter, I would have guessed—No, I shouldn't keep you standing out here in the hot sun, when I know your constitution is delicate. How thoughtless of me, after you have been so gracious in permitting me the use of your home. May I impose further by begging the pleasure of calling this afternoon? You see, I intend to plead for your assistance in entertaining my guests. Of course," he said, turning to Felice, "with Miss Bartleby nearby, I shall have to pry the gentlemen away to get in a day's hunting. *Enchanté, mademoiselle.*" Felice's hand was also saluted and also held longer than necessary, in Melody's estimation.

The viscount was instantly invited to take luncheon, tea, potluck supper while his own staff was getting settled in, anything the precious man desired.

"No, no, I must not intrude. And you, my dear Lady Ashton, must husband your strength for the houseguests. Would tea put too much strain on you?"

Would taking over Hercules's seven labors? Melody believed her mother would move mountains in order to have charge of the guest lists. An unsteady Lady Ashton tottered back to the Dower House, reciting names of local families and mentally eliminating any with marriageable daughters. Felice hurried after, most likely planning another stunning outfit to wear for tea. Any more daring and Corey would be served a rare eyeful, along with his watercress sandwiches.

Melody turned her attention back to the steps and Lord Coe's greatest challenge: Nanny. How infuriating that he found it so easy! All the viscount had to do was pull a bright red ball out of his greatcoat pocket. "Here, I brought this for Ducky. Do you think he'll like it?"

Nanny actually had to blow her nose! "No one's ever brought the tyke a gift." She snuffled, hurrying off to give her favorite his treat, leaving Melody in the selfsame situation she had vowed to avoid. How did it happen that she was alone with a practiced rake, a hardened charmer? She looked around to see if he was calling the birds out of the trees next.

Corey laughed, and the sound made her toes want to curl in her slippers, a not unusual reaction when he was close. "Don't think you can sweet-talk me so handily—" she started to bluster in defense, but he stopped her with a finger against her lips.

"Sh, kitten, I haven't said a word. Don't get your fur up, for I mean us to be friends."

"Friends?" she asked around the tingle in her lips. After what he'd last offered?

He took his finger away, reluctantly, it seemed. "It's possible, you know. You'll see. Trust me."

Trust him? She could trust a puff adder more! But his own sister was coming, and a friend sounded like a gift from the gods right then, especially a friend who was strong and kind and could manage whole armies of eccentrics without losing that devil-sent smile. Melody nodded, but with reservations.

Corey was satisfied, for now. He stepped back. "I brought all the children gifts, but the rest are packed up somewhere, except for the ball and this." He pulled a tissue-wrapped parcel from another inside pocket. It was a small china-headed doll, all dressed in ruffled lace. "Harry helped me with suggestions the last time I was here. Do you think Margaret will like it? Should I have found something else?"

The foolish man was actually unsure of himself! Why did he think little girls would be any harder to wrap round his finger than big ones? Melody had to laugh. Obviously, Lord Coe was more used to buying his gifts at jewelers rather than toy shops. "She will adore it, my lord. It is the perfect gift. Why don't I go fetch Meggie now, so you can give it to her away from the others. Say a half hour for Nanny to make sure she is spotless?"

Lord Coe met them on the path midway between the Oaks and Dower House. Meggie was holding Melody's hand, hiding behind her skirts. Melody tried to make introductions: "Lord Coe, this is Meggie. Meggie, please curtsy to your . . . your . . ."

"Uncle," the viscount supplied; that was as good a title as any. "Uncle Corey." He knelt to the child's level, one knee on the ground—another pair of trousers ruined. He could see the moppet had that same pale hair of all the Inscoe clan and his sister's turquoise eyes. Below that, she was wrapped in a heavy wool scarf. He gestured to the wrap and asked, "May I?"

Meggie nodded solemnly and stood still while he unwound the muffler. Then, "My God," he said, "she's beautiful!"

"Of course she is," Melody agreed, not adding

130

that any child of his would have to be. He was offering the doll, and receiving fervent hugs and adoration in return. Corey's eyes seemed suspiciously damp, and Melody knew there was a lump in her own throat.

The viscount swung the child up in his arms and exclaimed, "Heavens, Miss Margaret, you and the doll together weigh less than a feather pillow! Why, we'll just have to fatten you up, won't we, so you don't fly away in the next heavy breeze."

"Oh, Uncle Corey." Meggie laughed. "I can't fly away!"

Corey held the child close and told her, "No, my precious, I'll never let you get so far away again."

Lord Coe was in love. Irredeemably and unquestionably smitten, and by a skinny six-year-old with silky hair and a gap-toothed grin. All his plans would have to be rearranged, and now he couldn't wait for his sister to get to Copley-Whitmore so they could discuss the alternatives. There was no way this little fairy child was being sent off to Cornwall.

Melody's opinions were changing, too. How could she deny him the child, or deny Meggie such love? If his lordship proved at all trustworthy, Miss Ashton would have to relent. Then again, if his lordship proved at all trustworthy, she would eat her bonnet.

Father Christmas could not have received a warmer welcome at Dower House that afternoon than Viscount Coe and his carpetbag. His lordship presented Lady Ashton with the latest London fashion journals, Byron's newest volume, and a box of candied violets.

"These are just tokens of my appreciation for all of the trouble you have gone through on my behalf, and the assistance you have so kindly offered," Corey told Lady Jessamyn. He also permitted her to gush on about her plans for his house party, without committing himself to any. "There are still ten days before anyone arrives, ma'am. I should like to consult my sister's wishes before I send out invitations."

He turned to Felice and bowed from the waist. "But if we do have an impromptu dance party, or attend the assembly at Hazelton, I beg you will save me a dance, Miss Bartleby. I am asking now, of course, to get a jump on my friends and to avoid the crush of all the local beaux. Perhaps you would honor me by carrying my small gift." Felice's present was a silk and bamboo Oriental-style fan, with a not-quite-naughty picture of satyrs and nymphs at picnic on one side. Felice practiced attitudes with the fan—coy maiden, blasé lady, sultry houri—until Nanny told her to put the fool thing down, she was creating a draft on the tea.

Nanny would not ordinarily have been at tea, but Lord Coe had asked that the children be brought down. "Even Ducky and those savage little twins?" Lady Ashton was as astounded as if he'd asked her to dine with Hottentots or headhunters. Either might be preferable, for all she knew.

But Ducky was content to sit in the corner and roll his ball back and forth between his spread legs, and the twins were soon fixed in another corner, jabbering away over their gifts. Corey had reached into his satchel and pulled out two big floppy rag-doll babies with painted faces and two packets of ribbons. He handed Dora the doll that was wrapped in a pink blanket, with a pink dress, pink booties and a pink bonnet; with Melody's help, he tied pink ribbons in Dora's hair. Laura received blue ribbons and the other doll, all in blue. "There now," Corey beamed, looking at the others for congratulations, "now we can tell them apart."

It did not take ten minutes before each twin wore one blue ribbon and one pink, and each doll wore half the other's clothes. Pip and Harry were in whoops until Nanny clucked at them; they returned their attention to their biscuits and to the viscount's wondrous bag. Corey shrugged good-naturedly and vowed to try again, even if he had to tattoo the little heathens. He found another strawberry tart and popped it into Meggie's mouth, where she and her doll sat on his knee. (Yes, they were a fresh pair of trousers, and yes, there was strawberry jam already on them. No matter, Bates had already given notice. Twice.) Finally taking pity on the boys, Lord Coe pulled out his gifts to Harry.

"I know you said you'd be content if I just let you care for Caesar and hang out around the stable. After lessons and chores, of course," Corey added for Melody's benefit. "But I used to love this book as a lad, and I was as horse mad as you, I'll wager. It's all about knights and their chargers." Although he thanked his lordship politely, Harry wasn't quite as keen on that gift as on the other, a genuine leather jockey cap, which he declared bang up to the mark, the best gift he'd ever received, and wasn't Lord Coe the most capital of good fellows, Miss Mel? Melody was thinking somewhat along the lines of Greeks bearing gifts, but out loud she agreed with Harry's enthusiastic praise.

Corey held a leather box out to Pip. "P-please, my lord. Harry said you b-brought all those b-books from London just for me. I c-cannot thank you enough n-now, so I c-cannot accept any more g-gifts."

"Well, Philip, that's a fine way to repay someone's generosity, denying him a promising chess partner." Corey opened the leather case and regretfully fingered the carved ivory pieces. "Are you sure you won't reconsider?"

Pip looked to Melody, who smiled her encouragement. "I suppose I might, sir. B-but only as a favor, you know." They all laughed, Pip, too.

Still smiling, Lord Coe said, "Harry, I thought you were a better conspirator! I hope you didn't tell anyone about the last gift." Melody held her breath while Corey gently lifted Meggie down and, standing, brought the tapestry bag over—to Nanny! Inside were four hanks of the softest angora yarn dyed a lovely green color. "Harry thought you could use a new workbag, Nanny, but I hope you can make something pretty with the wool." Only Nanny saw his wink or got a good enough look at the yarn's color to see it was the exact shade of Melody's eyes.

Tea was over; the gifts were all parceled out. "But Uncle Corey, didn't you bring a present for Miss Mel?" Miss Ashton could have throttled Meggie as almost all eyes turned to her. Mama was reading one of the journals and hadn't paid attention to anyone else's gift after hers, and Ducky had fallen asleep. The twins offered to share their dolls with Melody, the boys were embarrassed, and Felice snickered.

Her face aflame, Melody started to reprimand the child for her rudeness, but Lord Coe interrupted: "No, Meggie is quite right. It would have been unforgivable on my part to forget the indomitable Miss Melody, as if I could. To my sorrow, her gift was too big to fit in the bag."

And that was a relief to Melody, who feared for a moment that the unpredictable man was going to pull a jeweler's box from his pocket and shame her in front of the children with a courtesan's gift. Now she would have to wonder for another day what he could possibly get for her that was too large for his bag of tricks. It was a surprise, he said, that she would have to go into the woods with him the next morning to find. If he was planning anything untoward, wouldn't he just be the one surprised, for Melody swore to bring Nanny and Meggie and Harry and Pip and . . .

Chapter Seventeen

Advance guards were dispatched. Melody sent the twins ahead along the path. Corey was delighted to see them each carrying a baby doll wrapped in its blanket, but for the life of him he couldn't remember which twin had pink and which had blue, not that he could rely on their keeping the designated colors anyway. He held his finger to his lips and shook his head, so the twins skipped back to Melody all giggly that they knew a secret, and she did not. Melody wasn't surprised that her scouts' loyalties had been so easily subverted and did not even think of sending Meggie to spy. That chit was firmly in his lordship's pocket, dancing ahead with a basket of sticky buns to offer him as a midmorning treat.

Corey stood in the clearing, sunlight on his pale hair, his coat slung over a tree branch, and his white shirt open at the neck. Melody caught her breath, reminded of her first sight of him in Barstow's inn yard when she thought he looked like a sculpted god. The crooked smile he wore today was all too human and all too manly for her suddenly racing heartbeat. In his hands, when her eyes got past the broad shoulders and the tanned vee of his chest, was her gift: a lightweight, twin-barrel, nearly recoilless, modern rifle, with embossed silver plates on the stock. A lady's hunting weapon, and all for her! To think that the last gift Miss Ashton had received was Mingleforth's *Rules of Polite Decorum*—and she had hit Lord Coe with it! Tears came to Melody's eyes, and she fumbled for her handkerchief.

"Well, I am glad to see that at least Harry and the twins liked my gifts," Corey teased to give her time to recover. Harry was wearing his cap and had likely slept in it, and the twins were clutching their baby dolls. They were, at any rate, until one of the dolls started to squeal and kick, demanding to be set down. First one and then the other piglet ran off, bonnets and all, the twins, Harry, and Angie in chase behind. Melody's troops were deserting her, and so was her willpower to resist Corey's enchantments.

"If this is some kind of bribe, my lord," she began, only to be brought up short by his laughing denial.

"What a suspicious lady you are, Miss Ashton. Didn't I tell you to trust me? The gun is only a gift, to show my appreciation for all you've done, and to atone for whatever aggravation or distress I may have caused you. I thought all women liked gifts."

Melody glanced quickly to Meggie and Pip; they were happily setting up the painted cloth target Lord Coe had also brought. "But it is much too costly. I cannot accept—"

"Now you are sounding like Philip. Don't be a peahen, Angel, I bought it for my own self-defense. Can't have you blundering around so close to the Oaks with that unwieldy antique you were trying to use. I thought I could show you how to shoot."

He thought he might give her pointers, did he? Melody walked over to the round target. "Come away, children, Lord Coe is going to teach me how to use the gun." Philip cleared his throat, and Meggie started to say, "But, Uncle Corey—" until Melody clapped her hand over the child's mouth.

Corey demonstrated how to load the rifle, speaking simply enough for Meggie's understanding, then paced off a short distance. No need to tax her skill, he said, just hitting the target would be enough for starters.

"Oh dear, yes," Melody agreed, trying to recall even half of Felice's affectations. Perhaps she could develop the other girl's knack of looking up at a man and batting her eyelashes. No, Melody was too tall. Instead she stood limply, permitting the viscount to position her hands properly on the rifle. Then he stood behind her, his arms around hers, holding the gun up. Oh dear, indeed! What had she gotten herself into?

Her back was against his chest, her cheek was brushed by the thin fabric of his shirt sleeve, her fingers were wrapped in his, and she was enveloped in the fresh lemon and spice scent of him. Melody never noticed that the viscount's voice was a trifle ragged as he tried to remember the instructions for aiming a rifle. Instead, she noticed how his words rumbled in his chest and how his breath ruffled the hair near her ear, so close to his mouth. Why, if she turned slightly . . .

"And squeeze back slowly on the trigger like . . . so."

The gun's boom brought Melody back to earth, that and the need to make sure her knees were still supporting her when the viscount withdrew his arms to check the target.

"We'll have to work on your aim, I'm afraid, if you can miss at this distance."

Aim? Had she been aiming? Melody smiled sweetly and wondered if she could try the next shot by herself, to get a better feel for the weapon, she said. The rifle was so light she overcompensated, and her shot hit the outer ring, which his lordship thought was just wonderful. He winked at Pip, who almost choked.

Melody fumbled the reloading, and then asked Meggie if she could spare two of the sticky buns.

"Shouldn't we wait for after the lesson, Miss Ashton?" Corey prompted.

"This is the lesson," she replied. "Ready, Pip?" She raised the rifle and called "One." The toss. *Boom* "Two." The toss. *Boom.*

Viscount Coe threw his head back and laughed, bowed to Melody, and brushed crumbs off his shirt.

If the viscount's intention was to confuse Melody, he succeeded. He did not behave like any London beau she imagined, idle and bored, spending hours over his dress and food. Nor did he seem to seek out low company for carousing or gambling. He acted the gallant flirt for Mama and Felice, the affectionate uncle to the children and, as promised, the warm friend to Melody. She just could not figure out why.

For the next few days, the viscount was everywhere. He gave the twins and Meggie turns riding in front of him on Caesar and oversaw one of his grooms' instruction of Harry on a docile mare. He asked Lady Ashton to accompany him on calls to the local gentry, in his carriage, of course, the one with the crest on the door. He played chess with Pip and discussed the boy's reading; he partook of make-believe teas with the little girls and make-believe teases with Felice. When he came upon Melody and Harry trying to mend the hogs' pen, again, he took off his jacket and started pounding fence posts. Corey could have called for one of his grooms instead of getting his hands dirty, but he pounded away in the hot sun until those pigs wouldn't have dared escape. He did not have to take Ducky for a ride or sit on the floor rolling balls with him for hours, and he did not have to accompany Miss Ashton when she went hunting.

Corey did not even bring along a gun, he showed that much confidence in Melody, but he did have some hints about training Angie, like leaving the impossible mutt home. The viscount wasn't patronizing at all about the woods lore he could teach Melody from his own experience, claiming he was only passing on the information because he was fond of rabbit stew. Naturally, he had to be invited to supper.

Lady Ashton was no longer wilted, Meggie was getting tan from following the viscount around all day, Pip was losing his stutter. The Oaks was getting ready for company, and Melody . . . ? Melody was feeling safe and warm and comfortable in his lordship's presence. At least she no longer turned to blancmange when he brushed close by her, or not often anyway. But why? When a spider cast its web, maybe it was looking for a place to dangle, not just a passing meal. When a noted rake cast his spells, maybe they were innocent, not necessarily insidious. Melody thought they were both likely instincts: the spider just spun, rogues just charmed, because it was in their nature. Well, she could admire a web for its dewdrop-diamond artistry without becoming any libertine's tasty morsel. But what a tempting trap, if trap it was.

Was it possible for a spider to build such an intricate, sticky web that it got stuck itself? Corey Inscoe came back to the Oaks every evening tired, dirty, and satisfied, to his own surprise. He played chess with Philip, raised Bates's salary, and relaxed with a glass of brandy on the library's leather sofa after everyone else had gone to bed, content to watch the dying fire and idly turn pages of his books. There were no balls, no all-night revelries or card parties, no greedy mistresses—and he did not miss any of it. At least not the greedy part.

Lord Coe still wanted Melody, uncomfortably more than ever. He had returned to the Oaks determined to use the time to his best advantage: to show Miss Ashton he was not a fribble and gain her trust. Hell, friendship between man and woman was just a temporary detour on the road to seduction, wasn't it? The only problem was, he liked her.

The more Corey saw of Miss Ashton, the more he admired her. Not just her beauty, although sometimes the sight of her, even ankle deep in pig wallow, made his breath catch. It wasn't as though she was exactly pretty; that little mantrap Felice was far more comely in the fashionable sense. But Angel had a freshness, a glow, and that dimple he'd move mountains and pig manure just to make appear. She would not go to fat like that rounded Miss Bartleby either; her shape when Corey had held her and the rifle in his arms offered promises—and another sleepless night if he didn't concentrate on Scott's latest epic.

There was more. He loved her affection for her ragged band and her loyalty to her rag-mannered family. She was honest and open. Why, if she disagreed with him, she would shout or throw things; she wouldn't sulk or cry or snipe at a fellow for two days after. She was intelligent and well read, interesting, and a good listener. She was not afraid to get her face in the sun or her hands in the garden. And she laughed. Not the simpering sound well-bred ladies were taught to make, but genuine, unaffected laughter. All in all, the poor confused viscount mused, Miss Ashton was everything a man could want—in a friend.

What a dilemma . . . and what in heaven's name was going on in the nether regions of the house? The servants had been dismissed an hour ago because his lordship saw no reason to keep them standing around yawning just to light his way upstairs, so no one should have been in the kitchens. Someone was, from the noise, and not making any secret of it either. Corey stepped to the desk and took his pistol from the top drawer. His soft slippers made no noise as he prowled down the hall.

"I am sure there is a good reason for this," he drawled from the kitchen doorway. "But do not stop what you are doing. Let me guess."

Melody nearly jumped out of her shoes at the sound of Corey's voice. Then she turned the color of dough that had been left out too long. Gads, what a hobble this was, finding herself exactly where she should never be, alone with a man—a semidressed man, at that, in his paisley robe—in the middle of the night. Her shaking hands continued their motions of scraping plates of food onto old newspapers, folding the papers, and putting the bundles into paper sacks. She knew her hair was undone, but at least her green cloak covered her and her lawn nightgown from head to toe. That fact gave her enough confidence to say, "Couldn't you just go back to bed and forget about me?"

"That's a contradiction in terms, Angel. I haven't been able to do it in months." He grinned when he saw the color rush back to her face but decided to stay where he was for the nonce, casually leaning against the door frame, out of respect for her temper and her aim. "I would have been within my rights to shoot you, you realize," Corey observed, putting the gun into his pocket. "Although I wonder if a person can be charged with breaking into his or her own house. Somehow I wouldn't have thought robbery would be your next foray into crime. Then again, most burglars head for the silver and jewels, not the pantry."

"Oh, do stop, you wretched man. You know it is no such thing. Mrs. Tolliver left these plates out for me to take."

"In the middle of the night? Now why, I wonder. Could it be that Miss Ashton is too proud to borrow food?" His voice grew softer, more coaxing. "You

141

know, Angel, if things are that bad at Dower House, we can still make some kind of arrangement. . . ."

Melody looked from the plate in her hands, veal marsala, to Lord Coe's paisley silk robe. No, she would salvage whatever dignity remained to her. She raised her chin in that gesture Corey prized, like a grande dame putting down an encroaching caper merchant.

"Yes?" he prodded, just to remind her he had the upper hand. After all, it was his house, albeit rented, his food, and her cork-brained scheme, whatever it was.

"Do you know that your French chef is the most haughty, self-important man I have ever known?"

"And here I thought I was. But no, I don't believe I had that impression of Antoine. Of course, I seldom converse with the fellow."

"Well, he is. You'd think he was the nobleman, not you. He has no concept of money and no respect for others less fortunate."

"Was that meant to be an indictment of the entire peerage, or just Antoine?" There was the dimple. Now that it was safe to get nearer, Corey started carrying the empty dishes to the sink.

"You see? Antoine wouldn't touch the dirty dishes, either. He has an assistant just to hand him things and clean up after him. But that's not to the point. The fact of the matter is, Antoine refuses to serve less than four courses, with removes, at a viscount's table. Anything less would be beneath him, or you. But you are only one person until your house guests arrive, and most of the food goes to waste since the servants have their own dinner before. And Antoine absolutely refuses to re-serve leftovers. That would be a sacrilege."

Corey was grinning by now. "Yes, I see the problem. But why couldn't one of the footmen bring the food to Dower House so you don't have to sneak around at night?"

"Because Mrs. Tolliver asked very nicely the first night, and your precious Antoine refused."

"He what? I'll—"

"He refused to let his labors, his artistry, his magnificent creations, his *leftovers*, go to feed the hogs."

"Ah yes, the pigs. I should have known. But what shall I do about it?" Corey asked. He was chuckling as he lifted two of the filled bags and her lantern, now that Melody was done. "If I order him to cook less, you'll have less food for the hogs, and if I order him to give them the remains, he'll either quit or feed me pig swill."

"Not to worry, I am teaching the twins French. Antoine will hand over the food just to get—What are you doing?"

Corey was raising her hood and holding the door for her. "I am seeing you and your booty safely home."

He wouldn't listen to her objections, and he wouldn't go back midway. In fact, Lord Coe walked Melody right to the kitchen door she had left unlocked in the back of Dower House. There he hung the lantern and handed her his two bags of foodstuffs, wondering how the pigs would feel about the glazed ham. With his two sacks and her two packages, Melody could not reach to open the door. "My lord?" she whispered.

"Thief-takers always get a bounty," he answered, and took his reward, while she had her hands full and her mouth open. Pinwheels, cartwheels, catherine wheel fireworks, Melody's senses were swirling and smoldering from his kiss, when Corey pushed her inside and closed the door behind her.

That was not a friendly token of affection at all. No friend's handshake ever left Corey Inscoe sweating and shaky, nor caused yet another restless night.

Chapter Eighteen

$\mathcal{W}$hy bother going to bed if you know you won't sleep? Lord Coe threw another log on the library fire and picked up his book of Scott's ballads. He must have dozed off, dreaming of heroes and wars and crowds screaming, for the noises stayed in his mind when he jerked awake. The fire was still high and banshees were still wailing. It was all of a piece, the viscount figured, taking the gun from the desk again, that the blasted house would be haunted; nothing about the place seemed to fit his notions of reality. The sounds were all too real, however, and coming from the front door. Fiend seize it, what if Angel was back, hysterical and seeking revenge? Let it be a banshee.

It wasn't. If there was one other feather-headed female in the world beside Miss Ashton who believed Dower House actually was, is, or should be, an orphanage, Lord Coe had missed the woman by minutes. What she left was tucked in a basket, crying as if the hounds of hell were after it.

Coe gingerly picked up the infant—no, he picked

up the basket—and the wailing stopped. He carried the whole thing back to the library to set it down while he considered his next action, and the shrieks started again. Not a slow learner by any means, the viscount hefted the basket and did his thinking on the move. Not that Corey had a great deal of deciding to do, for there was not a soul in his house who would or could know what to do about a screaming infant. Mrs. Tolliver went home evenings, and Bates would likely reenlist if Coe so much as asked him to hold the blasted thing so the viscount could dress. There was no hope for it, Corey and the baby would have to make their way in the dark, in still damp soft slippers, back along that wretched path, praying Miss Ashton was yet awake. He juggled the basket from arm to arm, trying to shield his candle and avoid jagged stones. Hell and damnation, he never should have left London!

The light was on in the kitchen, thank goodness. He looked dubiously at the item in the basket, wondering if he dared chance putting it on the ground in order to knock. The thought of facing an abruptly wakened household of screeching, swooning women was less appealing than facing Boney's cannons again, so he sacrificed his manners and his foot and kicked at the bloody door.

Melody was still wearing her green cloak when she opened the door, and Corey could see that her eyes were red rimmed from crying. Damn and blast, he thought, it needed only that!

"Don't you dare even think about—" Then she took a better look. "What in the world do you have?"

"Well, it's not another shipment of pig feed, ma'am. And no, it is not more evidence of my debauchery." Melody's bruised lips were enough of that! Corey avoided her eyes as he walked past her into the kitchen. "Some fool woman left it on my doorstep by mistake. Here, you take the little blighter."

Melody was even then lifting the infant out of the

basket and cooing to it. "Why, what a beautiful baby! And look, Corey, the clothes are fine white lawn and silk embroidery. This isn't some beggar's foundling. Maybe someone in the village will know what happened to the poor mother, that she would leave her baby."

"But that's tomorrow. What will you do tonight? I'm warning you, it does nothing but scream if you put it down."

"Poor dear is most likely hungry. There is no waking Nanny so late, and Betsy has gone home with Mrs. Tolliver, but don't worry, I have been around infants all my life. I know what to do. Here." She moved to hand the child to Corey, who jumped back as though it were live coals in her hands. Melody laughed. "I cannot warm the milk or find the bottles and those leather nipples Nanny used to have unless you take the baby. Or would you rather I put it back in the basket and chance waking Mama or Felice?"

Corey held his arms out, like a prisoner awaiting shackles. "No, silly, here," Melody instructed, cradling the babe in his arms against his chest.

While Miss Ashton bustled about in cabinets, Corey examined the scrap of humanity he held. "You know, she's not so homely after all, now that she's stopped squalling. She's got the prettiest smoky blue eyes."

"All babies have that color eyes at first," Melody called from the pantry. "But why do you suppose the baby is a she?"

"She's so light and pink and dainty. Look at those tiny hands."

"But all babies start out so sweet and delicate," Melody explained, coming over to look. "You're right though, she must be a girl; she's already smiling at you."

"Uh, Angel," he said, holding the baby out, away

146

from the wet spot down the front of his robe, "I think it's time we found out for sure."

No one in the village knew anything about a baby or a lady in distress, Betsy reported later that morning, but that sharp-nosed constable Mr. Pike was sniffing around about it, and he promised to call at the Oaks that afternoon to take the infant to the county workhouse and foundling home. Not if she could help it, Melody vowed.

Unfortunately, no one else thought she should keep the baby. Nanny shook her head and kept on knitting. "I'm too old for a young 'un, missy," she admitted, "and Ducky is already as much as I can handle, and he'll always need me. Don't look to your mama neither, for she's always been too busy being a lady to be any kind of mother. I can't figure she'll change now. Tigers don't change their spots, you know."

Lady Ashton merely asked if Melody had checked the basket carefully for an envelope or a bank note. Without compensation, the waif was just another orphan, and what did Melody think this was, a charity home? Felice, of course, had no time before the viscount's house party to tend to anything but her wardrobe and her complexion. She would not even hold Baby, for infants were so messy.

Harry moaned, "Not another girl!" and even Pip tried to show Melody in the books that they had no money for a wet nurse or a milk cow. Mrs. Tolliver had too many chores as it was, and Betsy too many mouths to feed at home, with her Jed out of work now.

Only Meggie agreed with Melody that the baby should stay with them. She even tried to give the infant her doll. "Because I have Uncle Corey, and Baby has nobody."

Mr. Hadley was no help. "No, my dear, I cannot sign the papers for you. It would be a life sentence, and the remnants of your dowry would never see you or the babe above dirt-scratching poverty. What

you want is a husband, girl, to give you children of
your own! If you take this infant you would never
have such a life, for no man would want such an
encumbered female. And think of your reputation.
All the evil-minded gabble mongers would spread
it about that the babe was yours, then you would
be subject to every kind of insult known. No, I am
sorry, I cannot let you take on another burden. Find
a rich man, Melody, then you can be as generous
and warm hearted as you please."

Melody did not feel warm hearted; she felt absolutely pudding hearted at the thought of facing Lord
Coe again after last night, after that kiss. All she had
to do, however, was ask him to sign some papers.

Unbelievably, he said no.

"I'm sorry, my lord, perhaps you did not understand. I am not asking you to support the child or
anything, just become the guardian, the male
guardian, of record."

He was pacing around the library in beige whip-
cord pants and a serge jacket, thinking furiously.
If Melody had another child, an infant at that, she
would never come to London. Besides, she was too
young to have such cares by herself. Damn it, he
wanted to make her life easier, not more compli-
cated. "I'm sorry, Angel, I did understand you, and
I cannot do it. You've been at such pains to bring
home to me my responsibilities. I couldn't just sign
a document and walk away. She would be my ward
forever! My way of life, my habits and interests,
they just do not include babies. I don't even know
what I am to do about Meggie, ah, Margaret."

"I haven't yet said you could take Meggie."

"And if you are thinking of offering me Margaret
in exchange for the baby, it won't fadge. You are too
young, and you cannot afford the infant." He stopped
his pacing at her protest. "No, don't tell me about all
the girls who are married with two babes before they
are sixteen. Half of them are dead before they are

twenty, and they have husbands to care for them. You cannot do it alone, and I won't help you."

Melody was stricken. So the hero had feet of clay after all. Why, oh why had she let herself forget he was nothing but a pleasure-seeking reprobate? "Spoken like a true nobleman," she sneered. "As long as you are comfortable and your peace isn't cut up, you'll write a check and consider yourself the most generous of fellows."

Corey's jaw was clenched, and Melody could see a muscle flicking at the side of his cheek. She didn't care; her own hurt and disappointment were too great. How could she ever have considered him a friend, and more than a friend? She continued: "I suppose you have your own standards, noblesse oblige and all that, until someone asks you to get your hands dirty."

"I have got my hands dirty, Melody." His voice was low, controlled.

She remembered him helping with the fence posts, carrying dirty dishes, holding sticky hands. "When it suited you, my lord. Thank goodness your true care-for-no-one colors showed before I made even more of a fool of myself. I was right the first time, you are nothing but a heartless flirt playing fast and loose with every woman who comes your way."

"Not every woman," he said with a deep breath, coming closer to where Melody stood fighting her tears. He stroked her cheek once with the back of his hand. "Come, we will work this out. My sister will be here soon, and Lady Cheyne. Between them they must know of someone who is pining away for just such a pretty little babe. Less than a week, Angel."

They did not have a week. They had less than ten minutes before Coe's butler announced there was a person, not a gentleman, mind, but a person, zealously and stridently demanding to see Miss Ashton.

Coe raised one brow and told the butler to show

the person in. "Unless you wish to be private, Miss Ashton?" Melody quickly shook her head no.

Pike waited for an introduction to the London toff and waited to be offered a hand to shake or a chair to sit in. He was going to have a long wait. His weasel face turned red, and he retallied all the insults he'd received at Miss Ashton's hands.

"I got you now, Miss High Boots," he crowed. "Waylaying a ward of the county and interfering in the rightful disposition of a minor under the laws of the king's justice. And I got papers."

Corey looked at Melody for an explanation. "It seems Mr. Pike, our local constable, gets a fee from the county for each resident of the local almshouse, which he also manages."

Pike never noticed how the viscount's eyes narrowed at the information. Pike was too busy demanding the vagrant child be instantly handed over to his legal care. Melody looked from his runny nose to his dirty hands to the hairs growing out of his ears and swore she wouldn't let him touch one of her pigs, much less an infant. If Baby had to stay at the county farm, temporarily only, then Melody would bring the child there herself. Pike waved his papers, and Melody crossed her arms over her chest. He threatened to have her arrested, and she offered to accompany him to the magistrate that very minute. Then Pike laid a hand on Melody's arm. Now that was a big mistake. Before he could say jack rabbit, the constable's feet were dangling inches off the ground, and his bony Adam's apple was bobbing over a rock-hard fist wrapped in his dingy shirt collar. An ice blue stare bored into Pike's watery eyes with the promise of unimaginable mayhem.

"The *lady*," Coe rasped, "said she would bring the child tomorrow. Was there anything else?"

Still dangling like a bunch of onions hung to dry, Pike gabbled out, "No." Nothing happened. "No, my lord."

* * *

Corey drove Melody in his curricle, a groom up behind, the baby in her arms swaddled in the multicolored blanket Nanny declared finished for the occasion. They hardly spoke beyond her softly voiced directions, and soon enough they reached the dry dirt track leading to the grounds the county set aside for its orphans and elders, its sick, drunk or crippled, its indigent homeless of whatever variety.

There were barefooted children poking in the ground with a stick and a scabrous old crone trying to get water from a well. A woman in a faded smock on a stool near the door coughed and coughed and coughed, and a bundle of rags issued wheezing snores. A man wearing the faded tatters of a uniform, with one leg and a crutch, stood propped against the wall.

While the groom held the horses, Corey helped Melody down. She clutched the baby more tightly to her shoulder.

"Who's in charge here, soldier?" the viscount asked the one-legged man, who merely jerked his head toward the house.

Inside was worse. The filth, the stench, a child wailing, people sprawled around like so many discarded scarecrows. "Who's in charge?" Corey asked again, and a scrawny hand gestured to a rear door. The soldier had followed them in, and now he added, "Dirty Mary keeps tabs for Pike, when she ain't shot the cat. She'd be in the kitchen cookin', if you can call it that."

Dirty Mary was facedown at the littered table, the bottle in her hand dripping onto the floor, where roaches and a toddler crawled. The one pot on the stove was scorched, and whatever it contained smelled so rancid Melody had to put her hand over her mouth. Corey led her out, keeping his arm around her and the baby. Unchecked tears streamed down her face.

"Were you on the Peninsula, private?" Corey was asking the soldier.

"Aye, servin' my country, and look what it got me." There wasn't even bitterness left in the man's voice, just resignation. He spit on the ground.

"Would you work if you could?"

"Aye, if anyone would hire a cripple, I'd work."

"Would you wash and sweep and carry water and see that these people get fed and bathed and, by Harry, treated like human beings?"

The veteran made a harsh sound in his throat that might have been a laugh once. "And who would pay for food and clothes and soap and medicine, eh, my lord? Pike?"

Corey reached into his coat for his wallet and pulled out a handful of bills. "I am paying. Pike won't be back, but you can be sure I will, with the magistrate. I was on the Peninsula, too, private, and I was proud of all the men who served under me. If a man let me down, he was out. Understood?"

The soldier saluted neatly. "You won't regret this, sir. And God bless you and your missus."

Corey helped Melody back up into the curricle and gently wiped her face with his handkerchief, then brushed her forehead with his lips. He peeled the blanket away from Baby's face and reached one finger to that so soft cheek. Tiny fingers wrapped around his.

"We have to see the magistrate anyway; a few more papers won't matter. But it's only temporary, mind, so don't get attached to the brat. And we'll do it my way. That means a wet nurse and a governess for Meggie and the twins while we're at it. As soon as my sister finds her a good home, Baby is going, is that understood?"

Melody gave a pretty good imitation of a salute, considering her eyes were watery and she had a baby in her arms and a big grin on her face. The soldier and the groom cheered.

Chapter Nineteen

*L*ord Cordell Coe was an experienced rake; Miss Melody Ashton was a green girl. She never had a chance. On the ride home from the poorhouse, waiting in the magistrate's parlor and showing Baby off, Melody admitted defeat. She tried to tell herself that her heart would not be broken when he left for London to resume his raffish ways. Her head told her it was too late, so she surrendered. Her virgin *heart*, that is. Melody acknowledged to herself that she loved Corey Coe and had a snowflake's chance in hell of changing his lust and liking into something else.

Melody conceded about the governess also, although Corey had been dictatorial and high-handed about hiring someone. That, too, was part of Corey's appeal, she realized, because he was right. Melody really was too busy with her chores to devote hours and days to lessons, especially when Corey expected her to mediate between Antoine and Mrs. Tolliver, to look over menus and invitation lists, bedchamber choices, and flower arrangements. The viscount did not wish to see his sister bothered with such details in a strange house for so short a time, if Melody wouldn't mind. As for Pip continuing to hold classes for the children, Corey declared that out of the question. The boy had too fine an intellect and had to be sent to school. He could study for the law or banking, where he could make a fine living for himself, or even the Church if he chose.

"And just how do you propose convincing Pip he would be happier among strangers? I have been trying for ages."

Corey just gave her one of those superior grins and said he was working on it. So Melody magnanimously yielded the point, but kept arguing until Corey practically demanded she find a suitable person immediately. Miss Ashton smiled, with no doubt that before too many days had passed she would see Miss Chase, her favorite young schoolteacher from Miss Meadow's Academy, here at the Oaks, willy-nilly. That was the way Lord Coe operated: he never seemed to be in question about what he wanted or scrupled about his means to get it. Miss Ashton could very well take a few pages from his book. She was young and lost in love for the infuriating man, but she was learning. . . . And she still had a few weeks to go.

Late that night, rocking Baby and wondering if the viscount was having as hard a time falling asleep as she was, Melody thought she heard noises downstairs. She went to the head of the stairs, intending to catch Harry on his way back from raiding the kitchen. But a light was coming from the little study where she did the books, so Melody picked up Baby and her candle, and went down to tell Pip to go to bed; he would ruin his eyes reading so late. Angie never stirred from her place at the foot of Melody's bed.

When Melody got to the bottom hallway, softly calling, "Pip," the other light went out. "I know you are there, you clunch, so light your candle and come upstairs." Nothing happened until Melody reached the study, when someone rushed behind her, shoving her into the desk, which toppled over. Melody protected Baby, but her candle went flying, right onto the pile of papers lying scattered around from the desktop.

"Help!" Melody screamed. "Harry, Pip, hurry. Fire! Up, everybody, up!" She dashed back up the stairs, nearly tripping over a frenziedly barking Angie, handed Baby into the first pair of hands she saw—Felice's. Meggie and the twins were shaking Nanny awake. As soon as Melody saw the children, Nanny, and her mother on their way out, she raced back to the study, where the old drapes were well caught, and one row of books was starting to burn. Pip was pulling them off the shelves and stamping on them, but Harry was standing in his nightshirt, open-mouthed, saying, "I didn't do it," over and over.

Melody shook him hard and shoved him out the door. "Get to the Oaks, Harry, get help. And take Angie. Her barking will get them up quicker." Melody picked up a rug and started beating at the flames.

Pip pulled the desk chair over and stood on it to tug the burning curtains off their rods, while Melody yelled that he was too close to the fire; they could let the whole place burn rather than take chances.

Then someone was pouring a bucket of water on the draperies, and someone else was shouting orders, and soon there were so many people in the little room that Melody could not breathe, for the smoke and the confusion. She dragged Pip out, past the row of men, some still wearing their nightcaps, who were passing pails of water from the pump in

155

the kitchen to the men in the smoke-filled room. Outside, Nanny had the little girls and Ducky in a cluster, and someone had put a blanket down for Lady Ashton to be prostrated upon, with Felice nearby retucking her guinea gold curls under a lace cap lest they get sooty. The dog was tied safely, but unhappily, to a tree.

Someone, the butler, Melody thought, handed her and Pip cups of water, and she drank thirstily, then went back inside after ordering Pip to stay with the smaller children.

Melody had to see if the men were winning or the fire, so she pushed to the head of the row and took her place, handing the heavy wood buckets to the viscount. She did not even know whether he recognized her or not, under the soot and smoke. He just kept encouraging the men to keep the water coming. Then, just when she was getting into the rhythm of the pass: turn, lift, turn, hand the heavy bucket to Corey, take back the empty, turn, hand it to the man behind her, the viscount swung around and stopped to call, "That's it, men. Fire's out, we can—"

Turn, lift, turn, hand the heavy bucket to—At least the bucket missed him.

Corey insisted they all stay at the Oaks.

"But your guests, my lord," Melody protested.

"Won't be here for a few days, by which time we can have Dower House cleaned and aired. I won't have you or the children breathing that unhealthy smoke. Furthermore, the Oaks is large enough that my guests will not be disturbed, nor are they paltry enough to be overset at sharing the house with a parcel of children." Corey had his doubts about some of the guests, that stodgy Pendleton, the dirty-dish cousin of Frye's, and Lady Tarnover's cabinet-aide stepbrother, but if they didn't like the noise and confusion of Melody's brood, they knew the road back to London, or Lord Coe could show them.

Lady Ashton and Felice naturally reclaimed their former rooms as if by right, the older woman bravely waving aside Lord Coe's sooty offer of assistance up the stairs. She would survive, Lady Ashton supposed, if someone could just fetch her some laudanum, and some hot water, and a little brandy to get the smoke out of her throat. The younger children and Nanny were put in Bates's care, to escort to the old nursery and make sure they had everything they needed. When Melody handed Baby to the impeccable valet, the viscount took one look at his former batman's expression and reminded Bates that they shot deserters.

The viscount's staff was thanked prettily by Miss Ashton and practically by Lord Coe with a keg of ale, then Harry, Pip, and Corey followed Melody to the kitchen for a general cleanup and application of the salve Mrs. Tolliver kept on a shelf. Bates had earlier brought down a dry shirt for the viscount, an armload of extra nightshirts, and a dark maroon velvet robe, which Corey draped over Melody's shoulders. It smelled of him, all lemon and spice, and trailed on the floor.

Melody and the viscount had a few minor burns, but Pip had been closest to the fire at first. He stood bravely while Melody dabbed at his face and hands. "Do you think we should send for the doctor, Corey? What if he is left scarred? Oh Pip, you were so brave, and you knew just what to do!"

Lord Coe turned the boy's face toward the light, the better to examine the burns. After what he had seen in the war, these were not so bad, and most were on the side of Pip's face discolored by the birthmark. "Leave the boy be, Angel. I think he will be proud to wear a few scars, won't you, Philip, when you go off to school in the Fall? You can tell the other lads what a hero you were."

Pip turned even redder, gulped, and nodded. Melody hugged him, careful of the burns, and sent a smudge-faced smile in Corey's direction, which had his lordship wishing the boy to Jericho. Pip did not comment, but he thought it peculiar how his lordship insisted on the formality of Margaret and Philip instead of pet names, but would call Miss Melody by her first name, or even the dog's name! Pip would never understand adults.

While Melody's attention was on the other boy, Harry was raiding the larder, fixing himself some bread and jam, wedges of cheese, sliced chicken, and blueberry pie. Corey found three more plates and a pitcher of milk.

With Harry's hunger partly eased, his curiosity needed satisfaction.

"I bet it was Pike who did it. What do you think, my lord? The front door was locked when I went to get you, so he must have used the window. It was open, wasn't it, Pip? Did you notice anything else, Miss Mel?"

"Is Pike that stupid, then?" Corey wondered, slicing the pie. "I thought I made it fairly plain that I'd beat him to within an inch of his life if I ever saw him in the county again."

Melody shook her head. "He's stupid enough, but not brave enough. Somehow I do not think it was Pike in the room with me. I do remember the window open a crack, but it was a warm evening, and I may have left it that way myself. And the kitchen door is always off the latch anyway. Maybe it was just a burglar." Melody did not think so, remembering those papers spread out on the desk, Mama's letters and ledgers, but she did not want to discuss her fear that the blackmailer was back looking for more information, not in front of the boys. Corey nodded in understanding; they would talk more later.

Meanwhile, Melody had a few questions of her

158

own: "Harry, why did you keep saying you didn't do it? *I* lit the fire with my candle when I fell, and I knew you were asleep in bed when I called out, so why did you think I was accusing you?"

Harry chewed and swallowed first, mindful of his manners, then said, "They always blame the bastard. Ouch." Pip must have kicked him under the table. "Uh, pardon, Miss Mel, Lord Coe. It's just that at all those schools, whenever anything happened, that's who got called up first. Sometimes it was easier to admit to whatever they wanted you to confess so you'd get sent home. Otherwise they'd get around to deciding to beat a confession out of someone, and you know who that someone was going to be."

Melody put her glass down. "Harry, surely things were not so barbaric! I couldn't let Pip go if I thought—"

"Philip is too smart to get into those situations, Melody," the viscount interrupted before Philip could change his mind. "In addition, he'll have my recommendation, which will ensure him a measure of respect. I think Master Harry was not such a scholar, and perhaps not always so innocent." Harry just grinned around a mouthful. "What I would like to know is why you did not simply say you were an orphan, Harry?"

"Why, that would be lying, my lord, and maybe even putting a curse on my parents. My mum is a fine lady, Miss Judith once told me, and pays for my keep. She never had to, you know. And I've even got a father somewhere. He was real good with horses, too."

"You never contact your mother, do you, Harry?" Melody asked uncertainly.

"Oh no, Miss Judith told me I never could, or she'd stop supporting me. I would have to be 'prenticed out then, or sent to the factories or mines. 'Sides, I don't even know her name. I always figured, though, that if things got really bad around here I'd find out and ask her if she needed a new groom."

Corey choked on a piece of pie, and Melody decided it was long past time they were all upstairs. They needed baths, and Baby would be up early, and they would have a great deal of work, getting Dower House back in order.

Corey disagreed. "You three heroes shall stay abed till noon if you wish. Mrs. Tolliver can look after Baby until the nursemaid comes, and I shall send the village girls to help your Betsy with the cleanup. Margaret and I shall manage to collect the eggs and feed the chickens without you, and Bates, I am sure, will be happy to assist the twins in feeding the pigs, if Master Harry here leaves them anything to eat."

"Old fussbudget Bates would never go near the pigs," Harry jeered.

Pip added, "Or near the twins."

Corey was pulling back Melody's chair so she could rise without tripping over the robe. "He gets to choose: the twins or Baby."

Lord Coe was more confused than ever. The woman he found more desirable than any in his life was two doors down from him. She would get out of her bath all rosy and warm—Zeus, he could just visualize her long legs and narrow waist—and she would put on *his* nightshirt. And her mother, her mother, by Jupiter, was *one* door down! Nobody's mistress had a mother! Hell, nobody's mistress had a houseful of orphans or chickens or pigs. None of which meant a tinker's damn, because Miss Melody Ashton was, in fact, nobody's mistress.

Nor was she likely to be in the next few days, with her old Nanny telling her to eat her greens, the village girls having a hundred questions, that impossible mother demanding Melody wipe her

160

brow with lavender water, some brat or other wanting a story. Worse, if Melody Ashton was not to be under his protection, then she was going to need protection from him and his reputation.

Corey was finally forced to the reluctant conclusion that Miss Ashton was not a bit of muslin after all. She was, indeed, a marriageable female, if a gentleman were so inclined, of course. He wasn't. Therefore, the viscount would not let himself be alone with her, or let his eyes watch her every graceful movement. He did not tease, did not brush against her by accident, he didn't even insult her once in the next three days.

Melody couldn't understand the viscount's coolness. He was polite, he was proper, and he could have been a parlor chair for all the affection he showed. After their shared experiences and the understanding she thought she had read in his clear blue eyes, suddenly he was a stranger.

Melody just couldn't figure it out until Dower House was nearly restored and Corey offered the ladies his coach for a trip to Hazelton to purchase upholstery fabric for new drapes. Mama and Felice were thrilled, especially when the viscount insisted on accompanying them and bespeaking tea at the best inn the town had to offer while Melody and Betsy were placing their order.

The fabric they selected was less dear than Melody had budgeted and temptingly near some lengths of damaged goods the linen-draper was trying to sell cheaply. All those fashionable ladies were coming to the Oaks, and it was Melody's own money, after all, from the dowry Aunt Judith left for her. She skipped all the rationalization; maybe the viscount would smile at her again if she didn't look like such a schoolgirl. The purchase was quickly made, a cream-colored silk shot with flecks of gold and green with only small water spots on one edge.

Next, Melody had one more brief errand before joining the others and watching the viscount fawn over Felice. She wanted to stop into St. Sebastian's, Melody told Betsy, to see where her parents were married. While Betsy had her own notions why her young mistress was interested in churches and weddings, Melody was checking the church registry.

There was the record of her parents' marriage, and there was the reason for the viscount's coldness. Melody laughed bitterly, thinking one might say she had been premature in her hopes for the regard of such a proud man. One might also say she had been premature in this marriage, if one were very, very polite.

Love. Marriage. A baby. But not necessarily in that order.

Chapter Twenty

There were good surprises in life and bad surprises. Finding a truly excellent old sherry that Lady Ashton had overlooked was felicitous. Finding that Miss Ashton's mutt was still prone to accidents in the house was not.

The new governess, Miss Chase, was a decidedly happy surprise for Lord Coe; realizing how much he missed the Ashton ménage when they moved back to Dower House was not. After a timid introduction, the schoolteacher from Bath turned out to be a pleasant, soft-spoken young woman who calmly tempered Felice's coyness and Lady Ashton's self-absorption. She and Melody shared a genuine affection, and the children were quickly enfolded in that warmth. From what Lord Coe saw of them, anyway. Now that Dower House was habitable, and Miss Chase had taken over the classroom with more formal notions of schooling, Corey saw very little of the youngsters. Astonishingly, he missed going up to the nursery in the evenings to watch Baby sleep or help read bedtime stories. He missed seeing Philip in the library at all hours or Harry in the stables.

What Corey missed most, of course, was Melody, and that was not a surprise to him at all. In fact, he had missed her before she left. While he was trying to maintain the proper distance, Miss Ashton had added miles. She was cool and aloof, conversing with Miss Chase instead of him whenever possible at meals, busy with the house or the livestock or restoring her papers to order other times. And no, she never needed his help. It was as if she were never home when Corey called, although he could see her, talk to her, almost touch her if he dared let himself, to shake sense into the peagoose. He was the one being careful, being protective. Why was she treating him like he had the pox? Didn't she know it was the man's job to back off a relationship grown uncomfortable? No woman had ever turned from Corey Coe, and it was a shock to find how lowering the experience was.

Even Bates noted his master was unusually blue-deviled and attributed the viscount's moods and megrims to postbattle fatigue, after the infantry's retreat. That would soon change, of course, with the arrival of real houseguests. Neither Bates nor Coe's London butler considered the Ashtons or the nursery party to be worthy company, although Bates had been caught out teaching Pip the proper way to knot his tie, and the starchy butler's white gloves were often sticky.

Corey decided he hated surprises. The incompetents in the Peninsular Campaign were always planning grand surprises for the Corsicans, and Lord Coe still carried the scars. When he was four his father had promised him a special birthday gift, then handed him baby Erica instead of a pony. Now that very same sister, the one for whose sake he'd gotten into this mess in the first place, wrote that she would have a surprise for him sometime

164

after her arrival. Corey should set aside another bedchamber. If Erica thought to lecture him on his duties and then parade another empty-headed chit in front of him like a filly at auction, she was in for a surprise herself: she could very well share her room with the wench. He wouldn't. Damn and blast, Erica was supposed to come, select one of the gentlemen, and be happy ever after. Corey did not want any surprises.

Now even Lady Ashton was plotting some disaster in the guise of a treat. She had come to the library earlier, interrupting him in some notes he was making for his steward in Kent, begging another bedchamber for yet another uninvited houseguest.

"Not that Barty's not invited, oh no. I have asked him to come many a time," Lady Ashton gushed over the sherry Corey was forced to offer. "He's been gone so long, you know, and now his ship will dock any day. The letter must have gone astray, for I wrote him of our little difficulties some time ago, but you cannot care about that. It's just that I cannot see him staying at Dower House. Not that I would mind having a man around the house, what with fires and people breaking in. But it's the proprieties, you know."

She tittered like a debutante, making Corey wonder what kind of queer nabs this Sir Bostwick Bartleby was, not to be trusted in the house where his own daughter lived, with Lady Ashton and Nanny. He knew there was some irregularity about Felice's birth, that the chit had never been presented in London, but he never cared to nose about for all the details. If the old roué approached Melody . . .

Lord Coe's face must have given away his thoughts, for Lady Ashton hurried on: "Oh, you mustn't think the worst of Barty. He's as sweet as a lamb."

A lamb that would be the black sheep in a family of cutpurses, likely, Corey thought, twirling his pencil.

Lady Ashton changed tack. "The Dower House is

so small, you know, especially now with that Miss Chase among us, and the infant and its nurse. . . ."

Weren't the governess and the servants safe from the man? Corey would be damned if he wanted the bounder around his sister.

". . . And right now dear Felice is the tiniest bit put out with her dear papa. As much as I hate to say it, I think we might all be more comfortable if you could see your way to giving him room here."

"Wasn't he supposed to be coming to take Felice to India with him? I would have thought she'd be happy."

Lady Ashton emptied another glass and fluttered her kerchief. "There's the rub. Dear Barty wrote that he wants to settle down here in England. A new beginning, a new family . . ."

A young wife. Corey got the picture and knew what it meant to Felice's future, and Melody's. The pencil snapped in his fingers. "I could see where Miss Bartleby might be downcast, but won't the nabob, ah, Sir Bartleby make provision for her?"

"He won't countenance her going to London until he has a respectable wife, he writes. The old scandals, don't you know. And he did mention how he thought she must have been a trifle extravagant recently, the naughty puss. I'm sure he'll come around, you know, if only . . ."

If only he is not subjected to a spoiled brat's tantrums, Corey concluded. He could well visualize life with a disgruntled prima donna like Felice, and he almost pitied the man.

Then Lady Ashton spoke the fatal words: "And if everything works out, I think we may have a happy surprise for you. Melody won't have to worry about this old house anymore, or all those children. We'll all go to London."

So this selfish, silk-clad sot was promoting the match, was she, to feather her own nest? Corey would give the old rakehell house space, all right. He'd keep

166

him so far from Melody the dastard wouldn't recognize her if he passed her on the street!

There are certain surprises that are known as ambushes. A weathered soldier learns to anticipate them, and a determined bachelor, hardened after a few Seasons on the town, knows the forewarning signs.

When no one was supposed to be in a bachelor's rooms, yet by odd scents and little rustlings someone unmistakably was, that spelled trouble. When the bed-curtains on the big four-poster were pulled shut in the daytime, only disaster for the unwary could lie within, the type of catastrophe that usually ended in screams, tears, hysterical mothers, and weddings.

Corey stayed in the doorway, mentally calculating the odds of this being another housebreaker. Nil. "Oh drat," he exclaimed loudly, "I forgot my book." He noisily walked down the hall, hiding behind a chest of drawers on the other side of the stair landing. Nothing happened, and the viscount was going to feel like a perfect fool if one of the maids found him skulking behind the furniture. He walked just as noisily back to his room. If the occupant of his bed was one of those same village girls hoping for a promotion, he could send her off with a smile and a smack to her bottom. But what if the intruder were, say, Felice, feeling ill-used and cast-off by her father, who saw a way to guarantee her own future? Ambitious and spiteful, Felice could never stand to see Melody take precedence. In one underhanded masterstroke, the golden diamond could capture herself a fortune, a husband, entry to London's most select doors, and a title, if Corey Coe were fool enough to get caught.

Zeus, what a hobble. He didn't want to embarrass the chit by calling for Bates or put off the inevitable by leaving, so he stood where he was and called, "If you are not out of there by the count of ten I shall fetch the housekeeper."

Nothing but sniffles came back to him. Hell and damnation, he thought, tears! Corey strode over to the bed, threw back the drapes, and started to bellow, "Get out of there this instant," when he realized nobody was in the bed at all. "What in blazes?"

Then two small, dirty, tear-streaked faces poked out from under the bed, and a little voice whimpered, "We're sorry, Lord Corey."

And another finished. "We didn't know it was your room."

Now Corey truly felt like a jackass, suspecting threats to his freedom the way a middle-aged spinster saw ravishers behind every bush. The only real menace he saw was explaining to Bates how there came to be so many dirty footprints on the bedcovers, as he gathered the twins close to him, propped up by the pillows.

"I am sorry I yelled at you, moppets. Now what is the problem? Running away from Miss Chase, is it? I thought you liked her."

"It's not Miss Chase," one twin started.

"It's Miss Mel," the other ended. "She wants to send the pigs off to market."

"To be killed."

By George, Corey was in trouble now. He took a deep breath. "But sweethearts, you knew the pigs had to be . . . sold. Pigs go to market, that's what they do, the same as little girls go to classes."

"But some pigs are too special."

"And should be kept home, with their friends."

Corey squeezed the girls closer. "Let me see, you don't want to keep all of the pigs, just a special— how many?" Each twin held up one finger. "Two. That doesn't seem too unreasonable. What does Miss Melody say?"

"She says we haven't enough money to keep any."

"Except the mama pigs, who will have more babies."

"But it won't be the same."

Tears started to fall again, and Corey had to shift

to find his handkerchief to blow noses. "But what can I do? Miss Ashton hardly ever listens to me, you know, and I think she would take it amiss if I told her not to get rid of the very favorite pigs. It's her business, after all. And I know she won't let me pay for their keep as I do for Baby."

Four big brown eyes looked up at him. His collar was tight. "I, ah, suppose I might tell her I need some special pigs for my country property. I could purchase the pigs from her, and then, ah, ask her to keep them awhile till they get bigger. Of course, I would have to rent some land back from her to keep them and pay for their food. Do you think she would swallow that?"

The viscount was nearly smothered in pinafores and petticoats. "I only said I would try, brats! But hold there, I want something back from you two hellions." Corey got up and went to his dresser. He fumbled in the carved wooden box that held his rings and fobs and came back with two pearl stick-pins, a black pearl and a white pearl. "What I want is a promise that you'll wear these for me, and mind you each only wear the right one. No one else has to know which is which, except us, if we are to be partners in this pig business. Agreed?"

The twins exchanged looks. "But Nanny won't like it."

"Us taking more presents from you."

"You just ask Nanny to tell you about casting pearls before swine, for you are my pearls beyond price. Now, how about if Dora has the dark, so I can remember that way? Laura will have the light." He pinned them on and kissed each forehead. "Now, let's go see if we can convince Miss Ashton."

"But what about the pigs, Lord Corey?" they chorused.

"The pigs? You mean the pigs are here, under my bed?" Two nods, two gamin grins. "Why, you little hellborn babes, I have a good mind to teach you

169

some manners!" He picked up one of the pillows from his bed and started chasing the nearest giggling, squealing little girl, then the other. When Bates and the footmen came with milord's bath some few minutes later, they were still at it, with flying ribbons and braids and feathers all over, and piglets rooting in the middle of the viscount's bed. Bates fainted.

The twins were so happy, Melody did not have the heart to deny them. "But there is no question of your paying for the pigs, my lord," she told Corey when the girls went to put their pets in the pen.

"No, there is not," he agreed, flicking a stray feather off his sleeve. "And I expect you to charge at the same exorbitant rate you got for the house."

"My lord, I do not put a price tag on everything."

"No? That's not the impression I got from talking to your mother. Rich old men, houses in London. If that's not mercenary, I don't know what is."

"And I do not know what you are talking about, Lord Coe. I think some of those feathers must have addled your brain. And I shall not let you buy those pigs."

"Miss Ashton, you are the most exasperating female I know. You'd rather starve than take my money, for which, incidentally, I made a deal with the twins so cannot renege, yet you would sell your very soul for pinchbeck security. Don't do it, Angel."

Then, instead of hurling missiles or insults, Melody did a very surprising, uncharacteristic thing: she burst out crying and rushed up the stairs where Corey could not follow.

Lord Coe really, really hated surprises.

Chapter Twenty-one

$\mathscr{I}$t was a house party from hell.

The first guests to arrive were Marquise and Lady Cheyne. Lady Cheyne took one look at Baby, being walked in a pram by the nursemaid, and decided Baby would make an admirable addition to the cricket team she was building. Lord Cheyne adamantly refused, declaring that their hopeful brood was large enough as is, and he had been considering his friend Corey's invite as a second honeymoon. The happy couple retired to their suite to discuss it and were not seen again for days except for meals, although loud noises could be heard now and again coming from their rooms.

Next came the Tarnovers, with Lady Tarnover's stepbrother, the politician. Lady Tarnover had deduced, somewhere midjourney, that she had not suddenly developed motion sickness but was indeed increasing. Her husband's solicitude set her teeth on edge, but if he was not within earshot she alternately complained or wept, which did little for Lord Tarnover's peace of mind.

The early arrivals reinforced Lord Coe's convictions that the state of wedlock was more a life sentence than a comfort and joy. Marriage was looking no more appealing than ever. Corey might be confused, and he might be disturbed, distressed, and altogether discombobulated, but he could always walk away from the situation, find a new bird of paradise and resume his carefree London life—as soon as this wretched gathering was done. Corey could not even find peace and contentment in his books, for the petty bureaucrat had taken the library over for his private study. Government business, don't you know.

Then Erica appeared, *sans* companion, nor would she deign to identify the unspecified houseguest.

Lord Coe kissed his sister warmly and made her comfortable in the sitting room, but warned her that he would put up with no matchmaking on her part. "Don't think to trot out some fubsy-faced female like you did in Bath. This party is for your benefit, not mine."

"My benefit? I don't understand. I thought you were inviting your old friends the Tarnovers and the Cheynes, who have been out of town so much lately." She patted smooth a coil of pale blond hair, very much like Corey's without the sun streaks, then her eyes narrowed. "Just who else have you invited, brother?"

Corey adjusted his collar and straightened his neckcloth. "Just a, ah, few others. Lady Tarnover's stepbrother was staying with them; he's something or other in the government. I couldn't very well not invite the man, could I? And did you know Peter Frye is thinking of selling out? He is nearly recovered from that last wound, so I thought he might like some fresh country air and exercise. Fellow officer and all that. He always admired you, you know."

There was a very pregnant pause. "And one or

172

two others," he muttered. "Frye's staying at his cousin's, and Dickie Pendleton's been hanging around the clubs. Poor fellow had no place to go."

"That's because no place is good enough for that stuffed shirt. However did you get him to come here?" His sheepish look was answer enough. "Oh, Corey, you didn't dangle me as bait, did you? That man has been looking for a female worthy of carrying on his elevated bloodline since before I was out!"

"Well, yours is every bit as elevated as his. You have a handsome fortune and, if a mere brother may say so, you grow more comely each year. I'm pleased to see you out of mourning, my dear, and I like that new way you have of doing your hair."

"What fustian, Corey, as if you notice how I fix my hair! You needn't hand me Spanish coin either, brother, because that horse won't run."

Then, as Corey lounged against the mantle under the portrait of Melody's Aunt Judith, his meek and mild sister proceeded to blister his ears. "You listen to me, Cordell Inscoe. I am not seventeen anymore, and you do not have the ordering of my life. You nearly destroyed that life years ago with your good intentions and your self-styled superiority. I was too young to fight you then. I can only forgive you now because I know you acted out of love and what you thought was for the best. But it wasn't, Corey, and I shall never let you come the heavy with me again. For all I love you, you can be autocratic and overbearing, you know."

"It has been mentioned. Also pompous, conceited, and a few other choice epithets you would doubtless consider good for my soul." He grinned ruefully.

Erica nodded. "I am sure that was a woman speaking, and someday I would like to meet such an astute and intrepid female, but for now, you seem to have invited every eligible *parti* you could get your hands on. I refuse to have anything to do

173

with them, Corey. I have plans of my own—no, I shan't discuss them now, until I see the child—so what are you going to do with all of your bachelors?"

"You need not worry about the numbers being uneven, the place is swarming with females, some of them even astute and intrepid."

"I am intrigued, brother, but now might I see Margaret?"

"I sent one of the footmen over to fetch her as soon as you arrived. But just remember what I said about any prospective mantraps, Erica. That guest you invited sleeps in your room."

Erica smiled, the same slow smile Corey had that started at one side of the mouth and worked its way around. "I'll remember, brother dear."

When Melody brought Meggie to the Oaks, she wanted them both to make a good impression. She need not have bothered, for Lady Wooster had eyes for no one but the child—turquoise eyes, the same unusual, lovely color as Meggie's.

"Oh," was all Melody could find to say, in view of the knowing grin on Lord Coe's handsome face.

The other houseguests drove up after lunch, and the fiasco was truly underway. Erica had, as promised, no interest in the assemblage, only wanting to keep the child near her, the child who was her duplicate in miniature. The rest of the company was too polite to comment, naturally, but Lord Pendleton's nostrils were seen to flare. When he realized he was expected to dine with the outré females from Dower House, his nose practically twitched like a rabbit's. He would not permit himself to be anything less than polite, of course, not even when Lady Ashton, with rouged cheeks and high-pitched, girlish voice, had a few too many refills of wine with her dinner and fell asleep over the sorbet.

Although he did not necessarily immediately comprehend what he saw, Major Peter Frye was a practiced observer. He considered how things stood with Lady Wooster, and he noticed how his friend Corey devoured the exquisite Miss Ashton with his eyes. Major Frye looked further afield for congenial conversation.

To Lord Coe's rather jaundiced view a few days later, it therefore seemed that things could not have gone more awry. The married couples were either bickering or in their bedrooms making up. Instead of finding a husband, his sister had found an illegitimate daughter she refused to part with, and of her prospective suitors, Lord Pendleton now had a permanent tic in his nose, Major Frye had transferred his attention to Miss Chase, the governess, and the politico had fixed his interest on Harry, of all things! At least Frye's cousin Rupert was taking on the role Corey had mentally preassigned the loose fish; it had only taken Felice's usual boasting of her father the nabob for the cawker's ears to perk up and his affections to be engaged.

Now the house was overrun with local gentry leaving their cards and paying calls, provincial beaux making calf eyes in the wrong directions, matrons pretending not to notice Lady Wooster and her butter stamp. This had to be the worst idea the viscount had ever had! Through it all, Corey had no one to laugh with, no one to help bemoan his matchmaking efforts, no one to share his concern over Erica and Meggie. In this whole crowd of people, Lord Coe was the loneliest he had ever been. His angel was gone, and he had no way of getting her back while this gypsy circus was in town.

Melody felt invisible. No one paid her any attention in the glittering crowd when the entire party from the Oaks was invited to Squire Watson's to partake of local society. Then she felt naked, as if they all knew her secrets, about the blackmail and the misused funds and her irregular birth. They were too polite to take notice, as with Lady Wooster and Meggie, but they knew. That was why the men ignored her and the women were either distantly courteous or outright unfriendly.

Melody could not have known that the local swains took one look at Viscount Coe's proprietary glare and decided to keep their distance, no matter that Miss Ashton was the most fetching thing the county had seen in ages. The older gentlemen felt it was safer to do the pretty with the married ladies and widows, the younger to get up harmless flirtations with that bit of fluff Miss Bartleby. Miss Felice was totally ineligible, of course—their mamas were frightfully provincial about such matters—but at least a chap could ask the little beauty to take a stroll in Squire's rose garden without fearing a heavy hand on his shoulder or that dagger stare in his back.

As for the women, there wasn't a female in the place who didn't see which way the wind was blowing. The single ladies hated Melody instantly for having won the race before the starting pistol was even fired. The matrons were taking a wait-and-see attitude. Not all was smooth in the courtship, obviously, but the whole shire was aware how the handsome viscount had been turning the countryside on its ear, firing constables, refilling the poor box at his own expense, and seeming pleased with these small diversions like supper at Watson's, and him a fine London gent. If ever a buck was marking his territory, the good ladies decided, it was Cordell Coe. For some reason, the viscount's suit wasn't prospering, despite the time he'd put in making up to those strange children at the Dower House, petting the calf for sure. None of the dowagers could figure it, unless that Melody Ashton had more hair than wit. If she was their daughter, they'd shake some sense into the chit all right, for scurrying away like a frightened rabbit whenever the viscount approached, sitting in corners or talking quietly with his sister and that mousy Miss Chase. Lady Ashton never noticed, acting more the debutante than her daughter, fluttering around in her gauze and trailing ribbons. The other ladies, meanwhile, found the muddled wooing better than a Minerva Press romance and were content to sit back and watch.

Melody thought she was keeping busy, seeing Lady Tarnover had a pillow behind her back, moving the Madeira out of Mama's range, reassuring Miss Chase that she was not making a romance out of whole cloth, that Major Frye truly appeared smitten. No, he would not mind that Miss Chase was dowerless.

"For you come with a fine mind and gentleness of spirit he cannot help but appreciate. And my understanding is that the major has an easy competence of his own. He has even undertaken some of the expenses of refurbishing the workhouse, I understand."

"Yes, he wants to do more for the returning injured veterans. What an admirable, high-minded gentleman he is," Miss Chase said with a sigh. "If I could only prove worthy—"

Melody cut the self-doubt off in midstream. "Isn't it fortunate how things have worked out? I was so despondent that I could not offer you a position in London as my companion, and now see, you are near to making a wonderful match right here in Copley-Whitmore."

"I know I have you to thank, Miss Ashton. Even if . . . if nothing comes from Major Frye's attentions—a female in my circumstances, you know—at least I am out from under Miss Meadow's thumb. Lady Wooster wishes me to continue on with her

177

and dear Margaret, and I would be more than pleased with the position."

Just then the gentlemen were rejoining the ladies, and Melody could see Major Frye headed in their direction. She diplomatically got up from the loveseat next to Miss Chase and said she thought Lady Wooster was beckoning.

That lady did indeed pat the sofa next to her, while Squire's wife saw her two spotty daughters fixed at the pianoforte, one to play and one to sing, for the delight of the guests not participating in the card games at the other end of the room.

"My dear, you are to be congratulated," Lady Erica said, nodding in the other couple's direction. "I think your Miss Chase is just what Peter needs, now that he has seen the world and war." Melody would have denied any credit for the match, but Erica continued. She spoke softly, not to intrude on the duet presently unraveling *Greensleeves.* "Now what about your own prospects? Forgive me for being outspoken, but Meggie adores you, so I feel like one of the family, and I sincerely hope for your happiness."

Erica also cared deeply about her brother's happiness, and she believed the two were intertwined, if only Corey would stop acting like such a nodcock. Why, right now he should have been sitting beside this intriguing miss, instead of trying to play a hand of whist and watch her every move out of the corner of his eye at the same time. Erica hoped the cocklehead lost.

Melody hid her embarrassment in polite applause for the sisters and smiled when Felice arranged herself prettily at the instrument's bench. Rupert Frye jumped up to turn her pages, and Felice proceeded to trill an Irish ballad.

"She is quite talented, don't you think?" Melody suggested.

"Quite," Lady Wooster answered dryly, noting

the doll-like blonde's arch look up at Rupert and her simpering smile for the rest of the company. "That one will see to her own interests, but what about you, my dear?" she persisted. "Do none of the gentlemen here please you?"

One pleased her all too well, in his dark blue superfine stretched across those broad shoulders Melody could see from here. Those were fruitless yearnings, however, so she answered Lady Wooster as honestly as she could: "I do not seek to marry, my lady. I find my independence comfortable and would not wish to become chattel to some domineering, high-handed male."

So the clunch had already made mice feet of it, his fond sister concluded, having no trouble recognizing Corey in Miss Ashton's description. She would cheerfully have strangled him for that shuttered look on the poor girl's face, but he was her brother and only a male, so what was one to expect?

"But a woman can only find security in marriage, and true fulfillment," Erica tried for her brother's sake.

Melody was astounded. Here was this woman, a widow who had flatly rejected the suitors her brother had brought for her perusal, who had a child born out of wedlock that she was determined to have by her side, who flaunted all of society's strictures, and *she* was advocating the married state!

"Forgive me, my lady, but I understood your own marriage was not entirely happy."

"Oh, that was my second marriage," Erica answered airily, applauding the end of Felice's performance. "Wooster was a pig."

"Your second? Then you were married before? And Meggie is not . . ."

She never got to finish the flood of questions or get any answers, because as Felice stepped down, that nasty, spiteful little witch tittered that it must

179

now be Miss Ashton's turn to entertain the company. Miss Bartleby knew well that Melody had no voice and could barely read the music, but her nose was so firmly out of joint that Felice determined to depress Melody's pretensions once and for all. Little Melody thought she could choose the ripest plum, did she, cozying up to his elegant sister in that insinuating way she had, leaving the gleanings to Miss Bartleby? Even the lackluster governess had attracted a wealthier, handsomer *parti* than ne'er-do-well Rupert!

At first, with all eyes on her, Melody just blushed and demurred. Then, when Felice called, "Oh come, Melody, don't be missish," Melody apologized to the company and sweetly advised them that she was looking to their well-being, for she had no musical aptitude whatsoever.

Felice issued the coup de grâce: "I thought all young ladies of breeding had musical talent."

It was Lady Ashton, after a few too many cordials, who mumbled loudly enough for everyone to hear, "That couldn't be true, Felice dear, or you'd—"

She was interrupted by Lord Coe. Throwing down his cards, Corey strode over to Lady Ashton and took the glass out of her hands. "What Lady Ashton meant to say was that Miss Melody's talents lie elsewhere."

The entire company was still; this was better than a Punch and Judy show. Melody was somewhere between horror-struck and hysterical. Lady Wooster patted her hand nervously.

"I am certain Miss Ashton is too modest to blow her own horn, unlike others, but she is a crack shot. As a matter of fact, to repay your generous hospitality and for your entertainment, I should like to invite everyone present to the Oaks in three days' time for a picnic and a rifle tournament."

The women were delighted at the idea of a picnic,

and the men were curious. It was Lord Pendleton, not surprisingly, who pointed out that it was not at all the thing for young ladies to be competing with weapons. Archery, perhaps, but never rifles.

Lord Coe grinned and his eyes sparkled. "Who said anything about the ladies competing, Pendleton? I will back Miss Ashton against any of you gentlemen!"

Chapter Twenty-two

*H*ow could he have singled her out that way in front of everybody? Melody would have done better to have thumped her way through some scales or sung Ducky's favorite nursery song, if she could have recalled it at that awful moment. She remembered the tune fine, now that she was home in her own bed. She also remembered every eye at Squire Watson's gathering being fastened on her, some in pity, some gloating at her discomfort. If she had just thought to recite a poem or something, her embarrassment would have been over by now, instead of having to be gone through again in three days' time, in front of the same group of neighbors and London sophisticates.

Melody's cheeks burned at the very thought of putting on a demonstration of marksmanship, having gentlemen wager on her prowess. She may as well tie her garters in public! If Miss Meadow got wind of such unladylike behavior, she'd choke on a macaroon and go off in a purple apoplexy. Even Miss Chase, when applied to before bed, considered the situation unfortunate but unavoidable without making the viscount look no-account. A shooting match was not what one could like, the school-teacher declared, but if Miss Ashton was going to do it, Major Frye wanted inside information to know what odds to back, and even Miss Chase had an extra shilling or two.

So much for responsible advice. Miss Chase was correct, however, about the viscount. He had stood up for her after Felice's troublemaking pronouncement, at least temporarily directing attention away from Miss Ashton's shortcomings. Therefore, she owed him the rifle match, even if it labeled her a hoyden.

Then Melody sat up amid her rumpled bedclothes and laughed. How could she lose her good name when she never had one? She had just been whining to herself how the world and Copley-Whitmore considered her no better than she should be, with all of Mama's "minor indiscretions." Let them. Melody Ashton was going to stop feeling sorry for herself and start having a good time. The London guests would be gone all too soon, and there would be little enough joy after that. If one in particular of the town crowd chose to place his wagers on her skill, meantime, Melody vowed to do her damnedest to see he won.

He liked her, he really did. He had stationed footmen around her house at night to guard against another intruder, and he'd made sure that Lady Tarnover's stepbrother did not stay around to cut up her peace of mind. The man had to return to London, pressing government business, don't you know. Melody had it from Harry, who heard it from one of the stable lads, that it was more like a rock-hard fist pressing up alongside his chin that sent the man scurrying. Of course, Corey could have been acting for the children's welfare in those instances, but he had given Felice a biting setdown on the ride home from Squire's, saying he would rather see the infants at his lawn party than a malicious shrew set on embarrassing his friends. Felice fled in tears, and Melody was still cherishing his words. Friends. She fell asleep with a smile on her face.

The next days were too busy to get into flutters over the match, anyway. Melody did not even have a chance to get Lady Wooster aside to ask for an explanation of that lady's enigmatic remarks about an earlier marriage. "You'll see," was all Erica laughingly teased before she tripped off to hand out the formal cards of invitation. Lady Tarnover offered to do floral arrangements, and Lady Cheyne took over Baby's care so the nursemaid could help Betsy and Mrs. Tolliver with the extra baking and cleaning. Additional staff was hired from the village, along with carpenters to erect an awning over the south lawn, in case of inclement weather. The gentlemen were hunting one day, fishing the next, to provide more delicacies for the tables and to get out from underfoot. Melody spent hours consulting with Antoine, and then she, the children, and Angie went berry picking, flower gathering, pig washing. Felice sulked, and Mama was prostrate from the exertion of checking the wine cellar.

The day of the picnic dawned on a perfect spring morning, crisp and clear and smelling of new-mown grass. The sky was as blue as Lord Coe's eyes, and the bird songs were as joyful as Melody's mood. She put on her prettiest gown, the white muslin with the violets embroidered on the bodice, so that no one could find fault with her dress. It might not be as suitable for target shooting as her father's padded hunting jacket, but what a figure of fun she would look in that! No one laughed at Miss Ashton today. They all thought she looked exactly what she was: a beautiful young woman very much in love with the man who made her eyes sparkle with his compliments and her dimples appear with his teasing and her cheeks turn rosy when he took her hand in his to greet the arriving guests. As for Corey, he had given up on his determination to keep his distance. One glorious smile from Melody had melted all resolve.

"Come," he told her, "for you are surely hostess here today. Not only is it your house, but I know I have you to thank for making it a delight for my company. I am disgustingly proud of you, Angel, and you haven't even fired the rifle."

No, but she was already reeling from the recoil.

Melody decided she was having the very best day of her life. The house was glowing, the lawns looked like a fantasy from Araby with cushions and rugs spread around, and the menu would have shamed a Carlton House dinner. Meantime, the children were as shiny and polished as the silverware and on their best behavior. Ducky sat on a cushion under the awning with Nanny knitting nearby, and everyone stopped to bring him a tidbit or a flower. Lady Cheyne sat with him and Baby and taught the little girls how to make daisy chains to wear in their hair. Harry presided over the refreshments table, and Pip was deep in conversation with the vicar and Mr. Hadley. Even Angie's coat gleamed from a brushing, and the favorite pigs wandered around, ribbons in their tails and soon collars of flowers around their necks. No one mentioned the you-know-what roasting on a spit for supper after the shooting, when the twins would be back at Dower House.

Melody's heart soared. When Corey served her himself from the food tables or brought her a cool lemonade or tucked her hand in the crook of his arm as they strolled among the happy, complimentary crowds, she felt as if she was two feet above

185

the ground. What crowds? Melody only saw his smile.

When it was time for the tournament, some of the guests, especially the older women from the neighborhood, chose to stay behind on the comfortable cushions and lounges set out. Mama was napping. Felice and Rupert were off on a stroll, and Lady Erica Wooster was nowhere in sight. To no one's surprise, Lord Pendleton loudly disdained to take part in such a rackety pastime. Melody did not call him a rasher of wind as she wanted to, for trying to ruin her lovely day, or accuse the pedantic popinjay of defecting rather than be proved a failure at what he himself considered a manly art; she merely directed him toward another path through the woods, where she was sure the scenery could not help but please.

The rest of the company followed Melody and Lord Coe along the path to the clearing, where chairs had been arranged a safe distance from the targets and tables had been set out with chilled wines and lemonade. Corey took charge, directing the contestants into groups and distances, ladies going first. There were three women beside Melody on the distaff side: Squire Watson's eldest daughter who giggled nervously, the Marchioness of Cheyne, and Lady Tarnover. The local lass was a passable shot, hitting the target with her four attempts, but the two London ladies were poor marksmen at best, leading Melody to think they were taking part merely to keep her from being singled out. She smiled her appreciation for their thoughtfulness as she stood to the firing line.

Melody's first shot was wide, catching the target on the outer circle. She could hear wagers being called, Lord Coe being teased for his boasts. She settled her mind to the task at hand and hit the center blue circle with her next three tries.

Laughing, Corey took the rifle from her. "Sweetheart, it's obvious you'll never be a gambler. You're supposed to lose the first round to make the odds go higher."

"But the ladies shoot at close range," Squire put in. "I'll still take her on."

Two of the local youths stepped forward and the rest of the houseguests. Major Frye winked at Melody when he took his turn, getting two of his balls into the blue. Lord Cheyne had the best round, and only one of the local boys managed to hit the target all four tries. The other retreated to good-natured hoots and whistles and Miss Watson's ministrations.

Lord Coe refused to take a turn, declaring himself impartial judge. Everyone laughed, and Melody felt her face grow warm. For the next round the target was moved back, and Lord Cheyne was declared winner among the men. Then the marquise and Melody took turns alternating their shots, both scoring four bull's-eyes. Wagering grew more enthusiastic.

"Much more distance would be unfair to Miss Ashton, with her lighter rifle," Corey declared, "so I propose a change in the procedure to moving targets. What say you, Cheyne?"

His lordship was game, so they called intermission while Pip practiced throwing wafers in the air, and the men cheerfully argued over Melody's advantage with the lighter weapon versus the male's natural hunting instincts and years of practice, to say nothing about wars and such.

Before they could resume the match, Lord Pendleton came blundering into the clearing, all red-faced and out of breath, his hair in disorder for the first time in anyone's memory, his clothing looking dampish.

"This is the most ramshackle household it has ever been my misfortune to visit, my lord," he in-

187

formed his host and anyone standing nearby. "I shall inform my man to commence packing immediately. You'll understand, of course, this is not what I am accustomed to, nor what I was led to believe. In fact, I feel you were entirely unprincipled in your invitation, and I shall therefore be forced to sever our acquaintance. Good day, my lord." He stomped off.

Corey shook his head. "I wonder what bee that fool got in his bonnet now?"

"I, ah, think I can guess, my lord." Melody hesitated, not sure of Corey's reaction. Pendleton was a guest, after all. Corey's raised eyebrow bid her continue. "Judging from the path his lordship took, I believe he may have come upon the twins, who begged to be allowed a visit to the pond on such a lovely day. The water is quite shallow and sunwarmed, you know."

"Yes, Miss Ashton? You interest me."

"One can only assume from his lordship's, ah, distress that he did indeed encounter the twins, who were most likely swimming. They swim the same way they do everything, boisterously and with great enthusiasm."

"And au naturel if I don't miss my guess!" Corey laughed out loud. "What a sight it must have been. I hope those bare-bottomed little urchins soaked some of the starch out of his stuffed shirt, but I doubt it."

"Then you aren't sorry to see him go?"

"Heavens, no. I am only sorry you had to be insulted by the prig."

Melody smiled. "Don't be. I told him which path to take." Corey smiled back, raised her hand to his mouth, and tenderly kissed her fingers.

Major Frye coughed and called for the match to resume. Melody's fingers tingled, and she missed the first wafer. Cheyne missed, with no such excuse. Squire and Lord Tarnover were busy making side bets, and Corey stated that he would cover any and all.

"Come on, Angel," he encouraged, and she never missed another.

After three or four of Melody's dead hits, Lord Cheyne cheerfully conceded, but Corey asked Melody to continue, just to show the company he had not been idly bragging of her skill. Harry loaded, Pip threw, and Melody hit anything at which Corey pointed. Then he was declaring her the winner and ordering champagne to be poured and placing a thin gold victory circlet on her curls. If anyone was thinking of other gold bands, they were too well-bred to speak their thoughts aloud.

Squire Watson wanted to know what Coe would have done if one of the men had been triumphant.

"I've seen most of you gentlemen shoot, remember, so I was not worried. However, if the little lady was having an off day or something equally as unlikely, for instance the sky falling in, why then *I* would have challenged the winner myself. Have to keep the house honor, don't you know."

Everyone was laughing and calling for a match between Corey and Melody, and she was looking at him speculatively. She had never seen his lordship shoot at all.

Melody was never to have her curiosity satisfied, because just then Corey let out an oath. The stem of the wineglass snapped in his fingers, and champagne spilled on the lace cuffs of his shirtsleeves. His face lost all color, as if he had just seen a ghost.

He had.

The whole assembly turned to follow his gaze, where Lady Erica was slowly walking up the path with an officer in scarlet regimentals at her side. He was seen to be limping, and his arm was across her shoulders. From the expression on the soldier's face when he looked at Corey's sister, his arm was not there just for support. Meggie danced along beside them.

When they were close enough, Lady Wooster announced: "Ladies and gentlemen, may I present Lieutenant Bevin Randolph, late of His Majesty's Second Cavalry."

"I thought you were dead." Corey spoke before anyone could greet the new arrival.

The young officer looked Lord Coe in the eye and addressed him as if no one else was there. "I was. That is, I was declared missing and presumed dead. When I recovered and found myself in a French gaol, I had no way of communicating with our forces. Later, too late, I was released only to discover that Lady Erica had been married. I know who to blame for that."

Corey, too, seemed to have forgotten the eager-eared audience. "You were gone, man. And you were young and penniless besides. I couldn't let my sister waste herself on—"

"On a mean-spirited old man who made my life a misery?" Erica put in. "Who wouldn't let me see my own daughter?"

"*My* daughter," Lieutenant Randolph bit out. "And I will never forgive you for that, my lord, nor for the way you settled matters between us in Scotland. You would not listen to reason, not even your own sister's sworn oaths that we were on our way back from Gretna, not on our way there. You knocked me unconscious and had me trussed like a hen, to be shipped out to my unit. My lord, you cost me seven wretched years, for each of which I have been waiting to do this." And he pulled his fist back and struck Lord Coe a smashing blow to the jaw.

Corey wasn't expecting the punch, wasn't even thinking of anything but what a fool he had been. His feet went out from under him and he hit the ground, hard. One minute Corey was seeing stars, the next Melody's green eyes, deep with concern.

190

He stayed where he was, finding the cradle of Melody's lap much more comforting than getting up and facing the avid crowds or his sister's long-lost love. While Melody used Corey's neckcloth to dab at the blood dribbling down his chin, Corey felt his jaw—nothing broken—and said, "Welcome home, Lieutenant Randolph."

Erica smiled and tossed her handkerchief down to Melody. "I can see you have gained a little sense in all these years, brother. We'll continue the discussion later, if you don't mind." She turned to go, the scarlet-clad officer's arm back around her. "Oh, there was one more thing," she said, giving Corey back his own one-sided grin. "I have had the lieutenant's bags brought to my bedchamber. Those were your instructions, weren't they?"

Chapter Twenty-three

"Why didn't the silly widgeon say anything for all those years?" Lady Ashton wanted to know. She had Melody pulling out every gown in the wardrobe. The nabob had finally arrived. Melody was trying to explain why they should put Sir Bartleby up at their own house rather than impose on Lord Coe and his sister at such a sensitive time.

Mama had slept through most of the startling events of the picnic and had seen nothing of the Oaks contingent for the whole day and night after. Brief close-mouthed calls from Lady Cheyne and Major Frye told Melody little, for if either of the visitors to Dower House had any more information about Lady Wooster's marriages, they were not discussing details, out of courtesy to their hosts and friends. Rupert came to call on Felice, but since he hardly knew the time of day, Melody did not believe he could shed any light on the situation. Who would tell such a rattlepate anything?

Melody had been wondering if she could call at the Oaks that morning, just to see how the viscount was getting along, of course, when Lady Wooster, or Mrs. Randolph as she must be, hurriedly came to call. Erica begged Melody's pardon for causing a scene and for keeping her in the dark. Now Melody was trying her best to explain the delicacy of the situation to her mother. It was like explaining diapers to Baby.

"Nonsense," Lady Ashton declared, making a face at the purple satin gown Melody held up for inspection. "They have a house full of guests right now. One more won't matter, and Barty don't stand on ceremony. No, that one won't do. I look like someone's mother in it."

Melody blinked. Mama *was* someone's mother, hers. Because of that, Melody felt she had to save the older woman from a possibly deserved setdown. According to his sister, Lord Coe was already nursing a dreadful sense of ill-usage along with a bruised jaw.

"But Mama, with Sir Bartleby at the Oaks, they will have to invite us to dinner; that's at least five strangers they would be wishing to Coventry, and Lady Erica is top over trees as is."

Lady Jessamyn shook her head. "Foolish beyond permission."

"Lady Erica? I think she was worried over the lieutenant's reaction to Meggie, that's why she did not want to tell anyone in advance."

"No, you peagoose. That gown. I look sallow in yellow. Whatever possessed me to purchase it? What was that about Meggie? They are going to take her off our hands, aren't they?"

"Yes, Mama, but Lady Erica could not be sure, earlier. When Lieutenant Randolph finally wrote to her, after he learned she was widowed, he knew nothing about a child. Once Lady Erica saw Meggie, though, she never wanted to part with her daughter again, so she was going to go live in Cornwall where no one would know the child wasn't Wooster's."

"But I thought you said she was married to that soldier, Melody. Hold up that pink sarcenet again."

"She was, but she had no papers to prove it, and if he chose not to acknowledge Meggie, she was going to reject him, despite all the sorrow. But he adored Meggie on sight and wants them all to emigrate to Canada, away from any gossip. There was another dreadful row, it seems, for Lord Coe wants to set them up in London, so he can share Meggie with them. Lieutenant Randolph refused to be so beholden to the viscount, but I believe they have compromised on some plantations Lord Coe owns in Jamaica, where Bevin, that's the lieutenant, will act as his agent. Of course, Corey made Bevin swear to bring his family back to visit. I'll miss Meggie, too, won't you?"

"The magenta? No, it's much too puritanical. I bought it when I was hoping to impress that toad Pendleton for you. Isn't there a figured silk in that closet?"

Figured? The gown had cabbage roses down its length. Mama would look like walking wallpaper. "No, I don't see it. Perhaps it got left at the Oaks by error. What about this pretty lavender India muslin? It would be perfect for a small dinner here, just the family, you know, to welcome the nabob, ah, Sir Bartleby home."

"Melody, you try my patience. I have not seen Barty in almost twenty years except for the twenty minutes when he first arrived. Do you think I am going to entertain him at this dowdy place and have those little monkeys hanging off him all evening? No, I am going to welcome him home to *my* home, in style, where there are enough rooms that we can have a private tête-à-tête if he desires. Without dog hairs on the furniture and infants bawling and

194

Nanny's needles going click-click-click every blessed minute."

Obviously, Melody was missing something here. "Mama, isn't Sir Bartleby coming to fetch Felice?"

"No, didn't I tell you? Barty is going to settle in England. He's discussing it with Felice up at the Oaks now. I don't know what's to become of the chit, after all the high expectations she had. I just don't think London will accept her, but I couldn't make her see that she'd do better with that nice boy Edwin at Mr. Hadley's office. Rupert Frye is an ivory tuner if I ever saw one, and after your father, I know the breed. He's only hanging about for the money, 'pon rep, which Barty ain't about to hand over to some here-and-therein knight of the baize table. Barty didn't get to be a wealthy man by bankrolling basket scramblers. Maybe he can make Felice see sense, for he doesn't want her living with us."

"Us?"

"Perhaps I should wear the ecru lace. That high waist won't show what he needn't see, although I've kept my figure well enough, wouldn't you say, Melody?"

"Us, Mama?"

"Of course, Barty always did like his women plump. Do stop that goggling, Melody. You look like a goldfish. Us. Barty and I, together as we should have been these twenty years past."

Twenty years? "But what about Papa? I thought you were so in love, marrying despite your families' opposition."

"In love with that feckless Ashton? Oh, he was a handsome devil and had a title, and we did think his father would come around in time. But I married the useless lobcock to spite Barty, pure and simple. We had an understanding, but he refused to give up his opera dancer till the wedding. That was Felice's mother. I wouldn't set the date with

195

any faithless whoremonger, so there was a big row-dydow right in the park. I was very young, of course. Got straightaway into James Ashton's carriage and convinced him how romantic it would be to flee to Scotland. I didn't know he found it politic to leave town right then because of the duns at his door. He thought *I* had money. Romantic, hah! The inns were damp, his horses were bone-rattlers, and we had hardly a pound note between us."

Melody sat down, dumping her mother's dresses off the chair and onto the floor to do so. "You eloped to Scotland like Lady Wooster? I thought you were married in Hazelton. I saw the marriage records there."

"We had to come live with Judith when I found I was increasing. Ashton was below hatches, for a change. Judith called the Scottish wedding a heathen rite and insisted on a grand, public, religious ceremony for the neighbors' sake. She also insisted on taking in Felice when the opera dancer left the chit on Barty's doorstep and his parents washed their hands of him except for buying his passage to India. Judith did it just to spite me, I always thought, though sometimes I suspected she had a soft spot for Barty herself. I tried to love Felice like Judith did, for Barty's sake, you know. The child could have been mine, but I was always glad she wasn't."

Neither woman heard Felice's soft steps outside Lady Ashton's door. Lady Ashton was searching out kid gloves to match the ecru gown, and Melody was too busy in her mind, blowing notions of her parents' storybook love affair to pieces like the wafers in the rifle tournament. They did not love each other; they were adolescent fools who spent years regretting their hasty vows. But they were married, over the anvil or not, long before Melody's appearance. She wasn't a . . .

"How dare you, Melody Ashton!" Mama was

thoroughly indignant, and not just because her dresses were on the floor. "What kind of woman do you think I am? I'll have you know your mother is a lady!"

The nabob was a caricature, thought Corey, in his upward-curving, pointy-toed slippers, baggy trousers, billowy silk robes, water pipe, and more rings than Rundell's. He was outspoken, overfamiliar, overweight. How could it be that Melody was too busy getting ready for this overstuffed mushroom to so much as inquire into Corey's well-being? She had to know his phiz would only frighten the children if he came to Dower House, so obviously she did not care. Hell and tarnation, now Corey had to entertain her would-be fiancé. If the blighter didn't stop puffing smoke in Corey's face and didn't stop crowing what a fine figure of a gel she was, he would be out on his fat ear in jig time. By Jupiter, Lord Coe knew what a fine figure Melody had, and the idea of this sausage-fingered caper merchant so much as touching her made the rest of his face look as bilious as his injured jaw.

"Do you think she'll have me? I mean to do it right this time, don't you know," Sir Bartleby was nattering on.

"Do you mean to say you've proposed before and been turned down?"

"Aye, but she was just a wee lass then, and I botched it. She asked if I'd be faithful, and all I could swear was that I'd try."

Corey could well imagine Melody's reaction to a philandering husband. "And now?"

"Oh, now I'd lie. Bostwick Bartleby don't make the same mistake twice, you know. Of course, it would be easier if I could see my little girl settled first, so as I can get on with my courting without reminders of past lapses, heh heh. I don't suppose you'd be interested? A fine gent like yourself needs a pretty armful to—"

"No."

"Aye, it's a sore shame, it is, but the chit's birth is against her. Of course, I intend to come down heavy for the right man."

"If I loved your daughter, sir, her birth would not matter tuppence. Without love, all the gold in Asia could not make me a tenant for life."

"Aye, Jessie warned you were a toplofty devil. Don't see what you young 'uns are about, dallyin' around, not that I did so well in my salad days neither. Still, there is Felice to consider. A rare handful, that puss. Pretty as can stare, too. No way I can take her to London with us, her being the image of her mother. Ah well, take one hurdle at a time, I always say. What about a toast? Here's to successful wooing."

Corey nearly gagged.

Antoine's fine dinner stuck in Melody's throat. She would tell Corey, she should tell Corey, but how *could* she tell Corey that she was not baseborn after all? A lady did not simply approach a gentleman after dinner and announce that she was not a bastard, that her birth was every bit as good as his own, and therefore ... and therefore what? And therefore he could tender an honorable proposal? Therefore he was free to love her as she loved him? Melody could sooner take her slippers off and dance on the tabletop through all five courses and removes.

The nabob would likely applaud, the old roué. If that overfed philanderer pinched her one more time or patted his lap for her to sit, Melody would box his ears. Could that enormous rock pinned in his cravat be a real ruby? No wonder Corey was scowling, the way Barty and Mama were carrying on like turtledoves right at his table. Perhaps this evening

198

was not a good time to seek a private conversation with the viscount anyway.

As soon as the gentlemen rejoined the ladies after dinner, a still glowering Corey asked Miss Ashton to attend him in the library on a business matter. Miss Ashton took one look at his forbidding expression and thought she had better remain with her mother, in case that lady's delicate constitution required a daughter's care.

"Your mother is as delicate as an ox," Lord Coe declared, grasping Melody firmly by the arm and leading her from the room. "And she has as much motherly instinct, if less sense. If I don't miss my guess she and that court card pasha will be off for a stroll in the rose garden shortly to decide your future."

Melody certainly hoped the infatuated lovebirds would get on with the formalities and make the announcement soon before she sank with embarrassment. The viscount nodded curtly to his sister, who was trying to hide her smiles behind a fan. Erica smiled encouragement to Melody.

"Mama is just a trifle excitable, my lord," she started to say when they reached the library.

"My stallion is a trifle excitable, too, Miss Ashton, and I keep him on a short rein. No, don't get in a dudgeon. I did not mean to insult your mother, and if I have to wish you happy, then I shall, although I wish you will reconsider."

While Corey poured them both glasses of wine Melody told him, "But, my lord, I have nothing to say in the matter."

"I cannot believe that of you. You have been the most outspoken, managing female of my acquaintance." He held up his hand. "No matter, that is not what I wish to discuss. Another blackmail letter has been delivered to my sister this afternoon."

Melody was shaken by that. "Oh no! Just when

Lady Erica seems to be finding such joy. Who could be so cruel? How did the letter come?"

"Sip your wine, Angel, you look too pale. No one shall harm Erica or Meggie, have no fear. The letter was in the basket with all of the other post and notes from the locals thanking us for the picnic. No one recalls the letter in particular. That's not important, nor is anyone's getting wind of Erica's so-called bigamous marriage to Wooster. It will be a nine days' wonder in London, till something else comes along. Erica wishes to forget about the threat and let the blackmailer do his worst. I spoke to your mother earlier, and she told me to let it drop, also. She seems to feel the nabob would know how to handle any awkwardness that might come up about the money or extortion threats."

"But we have to catch the criminal! There are other people who could be threatened, and people would keep on thinking it was Mama who's the villain."

Corey smiled for the first time. "I knew I could count on you, Angel. I, too, would like to see an end to this business, and I do not want to see my family affairs published in the broadsides if I can avoid it. Now that I have your permission, I can proceed to lay a trap for our scoundrel."

"Wonderful. When and where? What shall I do to help?"

His lordship sat back. "But, Melody, an outlaw rendezvous is no place for a lady."

"Don't be cork-brained. Of course I must be there."

Corey got out of his chair and came around to her side of the desk. "No, my dear. I know you are pluck to the backbone, but there could be danger."

Melody stood, too. "You know very well I can protect myself. I am going." Her determined chin came up, and for once Lord Coe was not amused.

"There are other dangers. There could be a messy

scandal with bailiffs and magistrates. You are not going, that's all." He pounded the desk for emphasis.

"I know what it is," she declared, pounding right back. "You don't trust me!"

"Hell, woman, it has nothing whatsoever to do with trust. I am trying to keep this thing quiet." His fist came down again, hard.

"Quiet!" she shouted. *Wham.* "What do you think I am going to do, yell it from the rooftops that you are planning to catch a thief?" *Wham.*

"You've already just notified the household and half the countryside, blast you for an interfering shrew."

"And blast you for an evil-tempered tyrant. I am going!"

"No, you are not!"

Now by this time the poor old desk was rocking. Pencils had long gone flying, papers were scattered. One more solid blow should see the decanter overturned. That final whack came as Miss Ashton turned to leave: "Then I hope the thief shoots you, and you die and go straight to hell." *Wham.*

Corey grabbed the decanter just as the door slammed behind her. "And I," he said to the empty room, looking down to see his lace sleeve trailing in the spill from the upended inkwell he hadn't caught in time, "hope the nabob has a very patient valet."

Chapter Twenty-four

So he didn't trust her, did he? Well, Miss Melody Ashton would just show that smug son of Satan a thing or two! She would take her good name, her first-ever silk gown, if she finished sewing it on time, and she would go to the assembly in Hazelton with the rest of the Oaks party—and she would flirt! Now that she was to have her dowry restored by the nabob, either out of generosity or a desire to get her off his hands, she could even simper like a debutante at her come-out. Yes, that's what Melody swore to do. She'd had enough lessons from watching Felice, and even from observing Mama flutter around Sir Bartleby. Melody would giggle and bat her eyelashes and hang on some man's every word, stars in her eyes and ... and rouge on her cheeks. She would go find herself some nice lad who liked children and dogs. Perhaps a modest landowner, or even a farmer, anything but a sophisticated man of the world whose emotions were as shallow as his hedonistic life. Her beau would have kind eyes and a pleasant face, but not be so attractive that he had an elevated notion of himself. He would have a sturdy, pleasant build without looking like some god every woman had to worship on sight. He would laugh and dance with her, and never, ever think that Melody was a liar or a cheat or a light-skirt.

That's what she would do, go find herself a husband. Why should Melody Ashton sit home on the shelf with only her dog for company? She was barely eighteen, and she had never been to a real ball. Just because some toplofty lordling did not trust her, she did not have to sit home weeping like some third-rate Juliet. Melody wiped her eyes. Trust him, he had said. But the trust was not to be reciprocal, it turned out. He wouldn't even tell her how he could suddenly tell the twins apart. He wasn't even her friend, and her dog was a more loyal companion. She sewed faster.

Melody's dress was finished on time, if her new mantel of cold-blooded manhunter wasn't. The gown was exquisite, falling in graceful folds that hugged her slim, striking figure. The bodice was a little lower than Melody was used to, but Mama assured her she would be out of the mode in a high-necked creation. In fact, there had simply not been enough fabric. That was why the sleeves were mere puffs, and the skirt was narrower than Melody would have liked. Tiny green leaves had been painstakingly embroidered over the cream silk wherever there was a water stain, and an ivory silk rose with three green leaves was fixed at the décolletage, bringing her charms to immediate attention. Another rose was fixed to the gold victory crown on her head, with her chestnut curls, shining from every potion known to a houseful of women and a great deal of brushing, gathered up and threaded through the circlet to fall in waves down her back. That was no angel's halo tonight, but the golden lure of a temptress.

The children were awestruck, even Pip beginning to realize how grown men could make such mooncalves of themselves. Mama never noticed Melody's appearance, fussing with her own before Barty's arrival, but Felice said something cutting about sparrows dressed up as swans, so Melody knew she must look as good as Harry said, bang up to the mark. Even Nanny said she'd do, and she'd better not. Nanny's gift of a gossamer-stitched shawl, made from the viscount's green wool and draped charmingly over her arms, made Melody feel even more like a Siren and less like a schoolgirl—if only her knees weren't turned to pudding.

The nabob simply pinched Melody's cheek as usual when he came to collect them, having quickly learned that Lady Ashton grew liverish if he paid fulsome compliments to any other female, even her own daughter. Instead of going into raptures over Melody's appearance, he bowed at the shrine of his ladylove's beauty. Mama's chest inflated with pride. She did not even hear her cavalier's corsets creak. She had found the cabbage-rose gown after all and made a perfect match to her gallant in his yellow pantaloons, red-and-black striped waistcoat, puce brocaded coat, and enough gems to make a dragon drool. If Mama looked like wallcovering, Melody decided, then her new steppapa-to-be looked like upholstery. That thought carried her to Sir Bartleby's hired coach, where she took her seat between Felice and Miss Chase. The governess had been convinced to attend the assembly, thus stretching the conventions, only after Melody's nervous pleas for moral support at her first ball, combined with Major Frye's entreaties and her own heart's desire. The major was waiting with the two carriages of the Oaks party at the main road, so they could all travel together for safety on the hour-long journey.

The hour was too short for Melody, who worried

that no one would ask her to dance. No matter, she wouldn't remember the steps anyway. Or she would stumble, or her hair would come undone, or Mama would overindulge in the ratafia. A thousand things could go wrong, like Viscount Coe not noticing her.

She need not have worried. Melody drew his eyes like the only candle in a cavern, except there were acres of people between them, many women more sumptuously dressed, most with more jewels, fuller figures, or more confident smiles. She was the only one he saw.

By the time the viscount could get to her side, the orchestra was tuning up for the first set. Damn, he thought, he was too late. That fat old fop would have her first dance for sure. Corey could not turn back without looking churlish, so he continued to where Major Frye and his cousin Rupert had joined their ladies. Corey was resigned to having the first dance with Lady Ashton. After the usual greetings, however, when he bowed over that overdressed old beldam's hand and requested her company for the opening quadrille, the nabob got piqued.

"Here now," he huffed. "That little lady is mine. I've been waiting twenty years for this dance, and I don't mean to be cut out by any jackanapes in funeral garb. This newfangled style of only wearing black and white must go with the sober-sided way you do your courtin'. Get on with it, lad, and leave Lady Jess to me. Frog bonnets, boy, the gel's like to die of embarrassment if you don't stand up with her."

The old fool was after Lady Ashton all along, not Melody? Angel wasn't going to marry this overblown bank account? The smile that broke over Corey's face could have lighted the darkest night. It did for Melody, blushing furiously, when Corey turned to her and said, "In that case, may I have the honor of the first dance with the most beautiful woman here tonight?"

"Can't," Bartleby called back over his shoulder. "I already do."

At which Peter Frye, taking Miss Chase's hand, chivalrously countered, "No, I do."

And his cousin Rupert, standing by Felice, could do no less than repeat, "No, I do."

All those "I do's" were sounding remarkably like a death knell in Corey's head, and the icy hand of fate was tapping him on the shoulder. No, the hand on his shoulder belonged to Jamie Murdock, begging an introduction to Melody. Murdock was a London acquaintance with a country estate somewhere hereabout, the viscount recalled. He was also darkly handsome and the very devil with the ladies. "No," Corey answered, sweeping Melody away on the first strains of the dance.

This was not Miss Ashton's longed-for country swain, no biddable boy who would never shake the foundations of her very being. This was Corey, and Melody shook. She floated into his welcoming arms.

The quadrille required concentration and movements between the other couples in their set, leaving little time for conversation. The viscount did manage to ask how long Lady Ashton and the nabob had been keeping company.

"Forever, it seems. Can you believe it? He really is a very kind man, and Mama seems much more lively since his return. I don't know how I can learn to call him stepfather, but I shall try."

"Has an announcement been made then?"

"Look at them. I think that is declaration enough." If the same could be said for another couple whose eyes never left each other, whose hands lingered over every touch of the dance's movements, then the local gossips could save another note to the London papers. Melody just kept floating.

When the next figure brought them together,

206

Melody felt she had to ask: "What about the letter? Have you captured the criminal?"

Corey did not want to argue, not now. He simply answered, "Sh, not tonight." Melody was content.

After the dance and a walk around the room on Corey's arm to greet the guests from the Oaks, Melody was pleased to accept the offer of Major Frye for the next set. Then she danced in turn with Lord Cheyne, Lord Tarnover, and Sir Bartleby, who performed every dance like an Irish jig. She was happy to sit out the next set with Lieutenant Randolph, whose injuries, he said, precluded taking the floor with the show of grace her beauty deserved.

"How gallant you are, sir, when you must know my toes are in agony and desperate for a hot soak."

Then it was time for another magical interlude with Corey, and her feet stopped aching. Dancing on clouds was never fatiguing. She wished it might be a waltz, on this her night of firsts, but the waltz was not yet sanctioned in the rural fastness of Hazelton. Corey handed her off to Major Frye, for his second dance, and excused himself. Perhaps the men were tired of their duty dances and were getting up a card game, Melody considered, for Lady Tarnover was sitting with Lady Cheyne on the sidelines, their husbands nowhere in sight. Now that Melody thought about it, Lady Erica and her soldier were no longer among those sitting on the gilt chairs, either. Melody looked around during the dance to note that Felice and Rupert must have gone out to the balcony, silly chit that she was, without a care for her reputation. Mama and Sir' Bartleby, who should have been watching, had eyes for no one else. Melody shrugged. It was not her concern, not tonight. . . .

After the dance, Major Frye led her toward the chairs where Miss Chase was now sitting, mentioning something about Squire Watson and a horse for sale. Melody's eyes narrowed. Not tonight? Then why was every one of the viscount's friends missing? Why all of a sudden were local gentlemen stumbling over each other to get to her side, when all evening they had been kept at a distance by Corey and his guests? They may have been the landed gentry and country squires she thought she wanted for a biddable husband, but not tonight. She made some excuse and followed Major Frye across the room.

Melody dashed into the ladies' withdrawing room and searched hurriedly for her cloak. Nanny had insisted she bring the green velvet so she didn't get her death of cold in that skimpy dress on the ride home. Now Melody wanted the wrap to pull over the white of her gown and her hair for some cover of her identity. She did not spot the cloak immediately and was afraid she would lose sight of the major if she dawdled. The night was warm enough, at least.

Frye was headed toward the rear of the assembly rooms, down an alley toward a building under construction. Melody waited until no one was nearby to see her, then ducked outside and around the other side. She could circle back without being seen by Frye or—yes, there was Lieutenant Randolph in his scarlet jacket, propped against a lamppost across the street, nonchalantly blowing a cloud. His back was facing her, so she darted into the shadows of the dance hall and sped down the dark corridor between it and a neighboring building, ignoring scurrying noises and the fact that her white gown was trailing in the alley's filth. She stopped when she neared the new structure, squatting behind a pile of bricks. She picked one up, just in case. The new building's framework was partially completed, but open enough for her to see Corey with his fair hair standing behind a half wall. He was making no effort to conceal himself or stay in the shadows;

he just stood there, his shoulders drooped, his head down.

Cautiously, Melody approached. "Corey?" she whispered, in case the trap was still to be sprung.

Lord Coe spun around. "You jade," he snapped out, grabbing her by the shoulders and shaking her till her teeth rattled. "What did you have to come back for, to gloat? Damn you, I let you get away once, now what am I supposed to tell the others?"

Melody tried to pull away from the madman; his grip was like iron, and he kept shaking her. "What happened? Did you open the satchel and discover the fake bills? Did you think you could just waltz back here and come the innocent with me? I saw you, damn your hide, in that blasted green cape of yours. You fool, couldn't you even have worn something less distinctive? What if Cheyne or Tarnover saw you in the street, you could end up in goal. Damn you, Melody Ashton," he cried. "I would have given you anything. You didn't have to steal it!"

"You *let* her get away? You idiot!" Melody had to break loose to go after the criminal. When she threw her hands up to break his hold, she forgot about the brick in her hand, truly she did.

Some few minutes later, Coe managed to pick himself up out of the dirt and give the whistle signal to his friends, who finally gave chase, after they stopped laughing.

The posting house, that had to be the thief's destination, Melody thought as she ran down Hazelton's main street. The dastard, she alternated, thinking she was it! The ball was the perfect time for such evil-doings, with so many people inside, no one out to see a lady in a green cloak. No one but a pig-headed jackass, she amended.

Melody's breath was rasping in her throat, and her toes were truly aching this time, for light dancing slippers were never meant for this hurrying

209

over rough cobblestones and uneven plank sidewalks. The pain in her side was growing, and she would never forgive that miserable makebate if the thief made it to the London coach, whose tin horn was just sounding as it entered town from the other direction.

Just a block or two from the posting house, Melody spotted her own green cape. She used her last burst of energy to close the distance between herself and the small female figure and her hustling companion. Wrapping her knitted shawl around the brick she still carried, Melody shouted out, "Stop right there, Felice, or I'll shoot."

Felice dropped the satchel and raised her hands, but Rupert hesitated. "You know I won't miss at this range," Melody reminded when he looked like he would snatch up the bag and Felice and make a dash for it.

"You wouldn't shoot," Rupert sneered.

"No, but I would," said the familiar, deep voice at Melody's back amid the pounding of many feet.

Chapter Twenty-five

*E*verything was tied up neatly, and everyone's future was settled. Everyone's but Melody's.

Felice and Rupert were being sent off to Canada with those tickets Lieutenant Randolph had bought in case he and Erica had to flee the country. The nabob wept into his yellow handkerchief when he brought Melody the news the next morning. Major Frye had quietly shepherded Sir Bartleby, Mama, and Miss Chase from the assembly, giving out that Felice had taken ill, and Melody was waiting with her in the carriage. Felice was not there, of course, and Melody had had to explain to the others. Mama swooned and Sir Bartleby blamed himself.

"It's all my fault for making so many promises. I never knew what to do with a chit except buy her things, you know."

Lady Ashton roused herself enough to go *tsk*. "Fustian. The girl was just like her mother, greedy and selfish through and through. How could she have done such a thing to me?"

"She said she wanted to get away," Melody explained, "where she would not always be the second-class, second-rate bastard stepdaughter. And she had no sympathy for the other parents who tossed their children away like handing castoffs to the ragman. She must have been bitter for many years. She also admitted she was downstairs the night of the fire, looking for more names."

The nabob had gone back to the Oaks to write one last check to his errant daughter. He stayed until the details were all worked out, and he could report back to Melody. She patted his beefy hand, and he blew his nose. "That man Hadley had to be called in this morning to transfer monies and things, and it seems the young fellow Edwin he took into his office was helping Felice gather the information. He says she made him believe some of the children just wanted to know their real parents' names. I don't know, the cub could have been under her thumb the same way I fell for her mother. I said I'd give him a chance after Hadley was all for throwing him out. Send the cawker to India to my partners. Always opportunity for a likely lad."

"That's very kind of you, sir. I don't think Edwin was truly dishonest; Felice was just so convincing."

"Call me Barty, m'dear, and perhaps you won't think I'm so kind when I say that we won't be going to London after all. Your mother is such a delicate little flower, you know, and this has been an ordeal. I'm thinking of taking a house in Bath or Brighton for the summer, as soon as she is well enough to travel, so my Jess can recuperate. Would you mind very much, m'dear?"

"Of course not, sir, ah, Barty. I think that is an excellent idea." It would be even better if the two were married before they went to scandalize another town, Melody thought, but she only agreed. At least Mama needn't be around when people started to ask about Felice. Melody had a hard time convincing Sir Bartleby that she had no regrets over London and no intentions of playing dogsberry to the lovebirds in Bath. "I am still needed here, you know. The children."

But Meggie would be leaving shortly with Lady Erica and her husband. Lord Cheyne had bowed to the inevitable, of course, so Baby would also be going when the house party broke up in a day or two. Pip would be off to school in a matter of weeks, and Harry was begging to be allowed to travel to Ireland, where Lord Coe had a cousin managing a racing stud for him. The cousin had written offering Harry a place, if he wanted to study hard to be a horse trainer. There was nothing the boy wanted more, and Melody could not deny him, no more than she could have kept Meggie from her parents or Baby from an idyllic home.

Miss Chase was staying on for a time with the twins. She was paid through the quarter, she said, but Melody suspected from the governess's placid smile that Miss Chase was biding her time while Major Frye settled with the War Office. Melody had an inkling he was thinking of relocating in the neighborhood where he was so involved with the poor and the returning veterans. She would not be at all surprised if he and Miss Chase decided to begin their family with a pair of irrepressible imps.

So everything was settled, and everyone had what they wanted. Except Melody, who would have Nanny and Ducky and a lot of pigs. And Angie. No one was likely to fall in love with the dog and beg to carry the mutt away, not the way Melody's luck was running. What she also had was a big bouquet of white roses with a card that read, *Please forgive me.*

In addition to the flowers, Melody had the memory of Corey softly kissing her last night in the streets of Hazelton, before he sent her off with Major Frye while he dealt with Felice and Rupert.

He was leaving in two days. Roses and remembering were not enough to last a lifetime.

She gave him another day before taking matters and a leather-covered box into her own hands. She did not stop in the parlor to greet the company or wait for the butler to announce her. Melody marched straight through to the library and plunked the box down on the desk.

Corey jumped up at her entry, took one look at the glitter in her eye and quickly moved the cognac decanter and glass out of her range. If he had been sipping courage from the bottle, it did not help his appearance any. One side of Lord Coe's jaw was purplish-yellow, while the other side was raw, red, and partially covered with sticking plaster. There was no way he could shave around that mess, so he had a seedy, shady look despite his elegant clothes, not helped by the dark circles under his eyes from another sleepless night, or their slightly bloodshot appearance.

Melody refused to be swayed by sympathy. Her heart was hardened against this rogue. She snapped open the lid of the leather case and announced: "Since I have no father or brother to defend my honor, I hereby challenge you to a duel."

Corey shook his head to clear it. God, she was magnificent when on her high ropes. No other woman of his experience could be so feminine and alluring, while behaving like a veritable Amazonian warrior, and sounding like a peagoose. "What about the nabob?"

"He has enough burdens to bear. This is between you and me, an affair of honor."

"Not even an affair yet, sweetheart."

She ignored the interruption. "Your evil intentions have been clear from the first. You have toyed with my affections, compromised me more times than I can count, even kissed me in public."

214

"And in private," he reminded.

Her cheeks reddened, but Melody was not finished. "You frightened away my beaus so I could not make a respectable match, and you cast slurs on my integrity. I demand satisfaction."

"I apologized for that, Angel. It was the blasted green cape."

"You didn't trust me even before that. If you had let me help set the trap none of this would have happened."

"I only wanted to protect you."

"You didn't trust me."

He ran his fingers through his hair, disordering the careful arrangement. "I never trusted any woman. What can I do to make amends?"

"You can meet me in the woods clearing, unless you are afraid."

He raised one eyebrow. "Ah, a challenge match. I confess I am curious, too, about which of us is the better shot."

"No, my lord, not a contest of skills, a real duel."

"You mean like between gentlemen?" The thought struck Corey as funny, and he chuckled.

Melody did not see the humor. She picked up the half-full glass of cognac and tossed it in his face. "There, isn't that the way gentlemen do it?" She stood with her arms crossed, while he mopped at his face with the ends of his neckcloth, painstakingly tied in the *trône d'amour* for the occasion.

"I should have known I couldn't get through a conversation with you with my wardrobe intact," he muttered into the linen. "But I do wish you would be more considerate of poor Bates and my pocketbook. I am already paying the man thrice what he is worth, just to soothe his nerves. I suppose it's a good thing you didn't slap me with your gloves. Knowing you there would likely be rocks in them." Corey reached over and took Melody's hand. He lifted it to his mouth and gently kissed the

215

turned palm, then he placed one of the pistols in it. "Here, Angel, you know I cannot shoot you. Do your worst. I deserve it."

Melody looked at him, all rough and disheveled, then at the gun in her hand. Her lips trembled. "I cannot."

"What's this, Angel, tears?" Corey took out his handkerchief and blotted at her eyes, his hand tenderly cupping her cheek. "You don't want to shoot me, sweetheart, but you don't want to marry me either, you know. I am just not husband material. You told me yourself. I am autocratic and dictatorial, and I would be jealous, possessive, and overprotective. You would hate it, just like you hated my not wanting you to help catch the blackmailer. I would want to wrap you in cotton wool, to see you safe."

"Why? Why would you care so much?" She stared intently into his eyes, looking for the truth.

"Because I lo—like you. We are friends."

"You let your other friends come into danger. You love me," she rejoiced. "I know you do! You are just afraid to admit it."

"Of course I love you, my Melody. You are the song in my heart, but . . ." But those carefree bachelor ways had been making one last desperate stand, thus the bottle and the bleary eyes. Without her, though, there would be no music for his soul to dance to. "But I shall try to make you a good husband."

Melody turned away so he could not see her smile. "You have not asked me yet, my lord."

His hand on her shoulder turned her around. "Do you truly love me, Angel?"

"Of course I love you, silly. I love you too much to let you grow into a grumbly old bachelor with no one to tell you your faults and no grubby children to lower your consequence."

He kissed her then, not as he would have wished,

216

due to his scratchy beard and sore face, but softly, a gentle promise. When he stepped back, still holding Melody in his arms, her green eyes were shining like emeralds in the sunshine. "I love you so much," she told him, "that I thought I would die if you went away."

"I was never going to leave without you, my adorable goose." And he kissed each eyelid for emphasis.

"But were you thinking of marriage this time?"

"Of course." She was grinning so he had to add, "You will just have to trust me on that. I take it that my suit has been accepted?"

"Hmm, I don't know," she teased. "Just how bad a husband did you say you would be?"

"Wretched. I am grouchy in the mornings, and I toss the blankets around all night. You would never need to worry about my straying, however. I'd be too cowardly to look at another woman, knowing your aim. But come now, madam, give me your answer. You have already shot me and doused me and subjected me to every indignity known to man. You have broken my nose and my chin. Don't say that you are going to break my heart, too?"

"Never." And this time her lips carried the promise. "Never, my lord, my love, my life."

Epilogue

The bride wore ivory satin and an antique veil. She carried a bouquet of pink carnations, blue forget-me-nots, and yellow columbines. The identical flower girls wore matching dresses, one pink, one blue. Another little girl was dressed in yellow and carried the train. The bride's mother wept.

The bridegroom wore white satin knee-breeches, white satin swallow-tail coat, white brocade waist, and snow-white linens. His valet wept harder.